The Great All-American Musical Disaster

A Farce in Three Acts

by Tim Kelly

I0591028

A Samuel French Acting Edition

FOUNDED 1830

SAMUELFRENCH.COM

Copyright © 1978 by Walter H. Baker Company

ALL RIGHTS RESERVED

CAUTION: Professionals and amateurs are hereby warned that *THE GREAT ALL-AMERICAN MUSICAL DISASTER* is subject to a Licensing Fee. It is fully protected under the copyright laws of the United States of America, the British Commonwealth, including Canada, and all other countries of the Copyright Union. All rights, including professional, amateur, motion picture, recitation, lecturing, public reading, radio broadcasting, television and the rights of translation into foreign languages are strictly reserved. In its present form the play is dedicated to the reading public only.

The amateur live stage performance rights to *THE GREAT ALL-AMERICAN MUSICAL DISASTER* are controlled exclusively by Samuel French, Inc., and licensing arrangements and performance licenses must be secured well in advance of presentation. PLEASE NOTE that amateur Licensing Fees are set upon application in accordance with your producing circumstances. When applying for a licensing quotation and a performance license please give us the number of performances intended, dates of production, your seating capacity and admission fee. Licensing Fees are payable one week before the opening performance of the play to Samuel French, Inc., at 45 W. 25th Street, New York, NY 10010.

Licensing Fee of the required amount must be paid whether the play is presented for charity or gain and whether or not admission is charged.

Stock licensing fees quoted upon application to Samuel French, Inc.

For all other rights than those stipulated above, apply to: Samuel French, Inc., at 45 W. 25th Street, New York, NY 10010.

Particular emphasis is laid on the question of amateur or professional readings, permission and terms for which must be secured in writing from Samuel French, Inc.

Copying from this book in whole or in part is strictly forbidden by law, and the right of performance is not transferable.

Whenever the play is produced the following notice must appear on all programs, printing and advertising for the play: "Produced by special arrangement with Samuel French, Inc."

Due authorship credit must be given on all programs, printing and advertising for the play.

No one shall commit or authorize any act or omission by which the copyright of, or the right to copyright, this play may be impaired.
No one shall make any changes in this play for the purpose of production.
Publication of this play does not imply availability for performance. Both amateurs and professionals considering a production are strongly advised in their own interests to apply to Samuel French, Inc., for written permission before starting rehearsals, advertising, or booking a theatre.
No part of this book may be reproduced, stored in a retrieval system, or transmitted in any form, by any means, now known or yet to be invented, including mechanical, electronic, photocopying, recording, videotaping, or otherwise, without the prior written permission of the publisher.

ISBN 978-0-87440-804-1   Printed in U.S.A.   #B1121

Written For a Flexible Cast of Twenty-Eight,
Approximately 18F, 10M, plus Extras

CAST OF CHARACTERS
(In order of appearance)

ETHEL KENT, *private secretary, capable and wise*

GINGER, *telephone receptionist*

JUNIOR DOVER, JR., *film producer. Young, brash, always
on the edge of disaster*

CARMEL McGREGOR, *an aspiring screenwriter*

SYLVIA METROLAND, *Hollywood's leading film reporter*

CHUCKLES LAFOON, *funniest lady in show business—or
else!*

BRONCO WHINNY, *a cowboy star protective of his "image"*

APASSIONATTA ABALONE, *a forgotten old-time star. Only
the films have gotten smaller, not her "talent"*

MRS. BUMBLE, *a "stage mother" and financier*

BABY BERNICE, *her obnoxious "child star" daughter*

TELEVISION ANNOUNCER, *works for a channel with "a
direct line to the stars"*

WINIFRED LUNG, *a drama coach*

PLATO VOLTAIRE, *a hack director, convinced he's a genius*

MAID, *works for Gee-Gee*

GEE-GEE FONTAINE, *gorgeous actress. Body of a goddess,
voice of a mouse*

3

GRETA GUTT, *Hollywood's toughest agent*

BOB EVERLOVE, *America's "Boy Next Door"—if the boy next door is a fathead*

SALLY, *a film enthusiast*

PAULINE, *another*

MAP SELLER, *a Hollywood institution*

TOURIST GUIDE, *another*

ASSISTANT DIRECTOR, *helps Voltaire*

CAMERA OPERATOR, *film crew member*

SCRIPT PERSON, *film crew member*

FLINT WORMWOOD, *macho type, specializes in police roles*

THEO BARTOK, *star of horror films*

MAKEUP ARTIST, *film crew member*

MUSICIAN, *Apassionatta's "mood-setter"*

EXTRAS, *tourists, fans, servants, etc., as desired*

SYNOPSIS OF SCENES

ACT ONE

Scene One:

Executive offices of DOVER'S EXTRA-SUPER COLOSSAL FILMS, INC. — HOME OF THE STARS.

Scene Two:

The same. Few days later.

ACT TWO

Scene One:

A sound stage.

Scene Two:

In the Writers' Building.

ACT THREE

Scene One:

Rabinowitz's Shanghai Palace. Sneak preview night, months later.

Scene Two:

The sound stage, some weeks after the preview.

SUGGESTIONS

Gee-Gee's "mouse voice" might be too difficult in some cases to sustain. The important thing is that she be heard LOUD and CLEAR. If her "mouse voice" presents problems, then any odd-sounding impersonation will work—flat Brooklynese, a twang, etc. Whatever is adopted, it should be a funny, unusual sound. The dialogue throughout the script should be delivered fast and crisp. No slow spots. This will require some special attention, because clarity mustn't be lost. Each "character" must be unique. Each completely different from the other, so performers will have to work on gestures, accents, etc. that belong solely to the characterization. Keep the show moving at a fast clip. There must be no waits between scenes. Nothing kills farce faster than "pauses." The stage properties described are down to the bare minimum for easy shifts. Director may wish to elaborate, e.g. "the *salon* sequence." If some flats are used, be certain they can be struck quickly and quietly. If an old (or new) camera for the sound stage filming can't be obtained a video cassette camera will work, or a TV camera borrowed from a local station. If not, simply design a motion picture camera with either light wood or carton boxes painted black. Nice bit is to have the lobby decorated with movie posters, and the ticket-takers dressed as movie theatre ushers. Director may wish to cut the business of the stars appearing at the sneak preview with arm slings, wheelchair, crutches, etc. If so, simply rework or cut lines referring to the "fight."

The Great All-American Musical Disaster

ACT ONE

SCENE 1

SETTING: *Executive offices of "Dover's Extra-Super Co-lossal Films, Inc. —Home of the Stars."*
RIGHT CENTER *there is a long table with piles of scripts. Behind the table a chair and a high wide dressing screen or advertising board decorated with movie posters.* LEFT *of table,* UPSTAGE, *is a desk and chair. On the desk is a telephone, usual secretarial props.* LEFT CENTER *there is a couch.*
Entrance from outer office is DOWN LEFT. *There's an exit* DOWN RIGHT.

AT RISE: TELEPHONE RINGS. ETHEL, *the film company's all-round "Woman Friday" is standing at the table sorting scripts. She crosses to the telephone, picking it up on the fourth* RING.

ETHEL. This is a recording. You have reached the executive offices of "Dover's Extra-Super Colossal Films, Inc.*, Home of the Stars." Ethel Kent, private secretary to Mr. Dover, Junior, here. (*Checks wristwatch*) We can spare you exactly thirty seconds. When you hear the sound of the bleep commence speaking. (*Pause*) Bleep. (*She hangs up.* GINGER, *a secretary,* ENTERS DOWN LEFT)
GINGER. I don't know if I'm cut out for this kind of

---

*Inc. in the play is pronounced "Ink"—never "incorporated."

work. (*Holds up the messages*) I take all the calls and I write down the messages.

ETHEL. (*Moves* DOWNSTAGE) That's what you're here for.

GINGER. The callers are rude. It isn't as if *I* owed them money. (ETHEL *takes messages, checks them*) The top one's from Mr. Jimson at the Projectionists' Union. Said he could play volley ball with that check Mr. Dover, Junior, sent him.

ETHEL. I'll attend to it.

GINGER. Laundry won't give back his shirts until he pays them for last month's fluff and dry. The man said it looked to him like Mr. Dover, Junior, was all washed up.

ETHEL. In this town everyone has to be a comedian. There's been a foul-up at the bank. Easily corrected.

GINGER. I thought working in a big film studio would be glamorous.

ETHEL. It's hard work. That's what most people don't understand.

GINGER. I don't mind work. What I'm worried about is my paycheck.

ETHEL. Shame on you, Ginger. Has there ever been a week when you haven't been paid?

GINGER. I wouldn't know. I haven't worked here a week. (GINGER EXITS DOWN LEFT *as* JUNIOR DOVER ENTERS *hurriedly* DOWN RIGHT)

JUNIOR. I don't think he saw me. I was too quick for him. (*He goes behind the table, sits.* JUNIOR *is a rather good-looking young man. Brash, impulsive, daring, hyper-active—always teetering on the edge of panic and ruin. His youth "might" excuse some of his bravado, energy and push—but chances are he'll be equally as incorrigible in later life as he is now, for he is a victim of that disease for which there is no known cure—*HOLLY-WOODITIS. *He is dressed in the latest expensive casual style*)

ETHEL. Who are you trying to get away from this time?

JUNIOR. It's a man who insists I gave him a bum check.

ETHEL. That could be almost any citizen.

JUNIOR. Fun-ee! Fun-ee! (*Puts his feet on the desk*)

Remind me to fire you. (ETHEL *is about Junior's age. She only appears older because she's more logical, practical and much calmer. Despite her almost constant irritation with Junior, she is genuinely fond of him, and can't imagine working for anyone else. Her frequent caustic remarks are a defense against the mad world of filmmaking.* JUNIOR *has to rely on* ETHEL *more than he cares to admit. She's his anchor in troubled waters. Although he doesn't show it on the surface, he is genuinely fond of her, too*)

ETHEL. You can't fire me.

JUNIOR. Why not?

ETHEL. You owe me too much in back salary. When I think of the reputation this studio once held. All the wonderful films your father created.

JUNIOR. (*Stands*) Don't start that again. You know how sensitive I am.

ETHEL. I do?

JUNIOR. I don't understand why my films never make a penny. They're witty—tasteful—artistic.

ETHEL. The last picture you produced was ZOMBIES OF THE STRATOSPHERE. Would you mind telling me what was witty, tasteful and artistic about that bomb?

JUNIOR. Give me a minute.

ETHEL. Why?

JUNIOR. To think of something.

ETHEL. You're all wrapped up in this new project. A disaster film. Where are you going to get the money?

JUNIOR. I'm seeing Mr. Bumble from the Bumble Bank of Burbank this morning.

ETHEL. He probably wants to collect the money *you owe him.*

JUNIOR. He was quite impressed when I told him about my new project.

ETHEL. No one wants to see another disaster film. They're *passé.* They've been *passé* for years. Why don't you come up with something new?

JUNIOR. ZOMBIES was new.

ETHEL. Ha! The critics said the idea was so old the ushers had to wipe the screen with a dust cloth.

JUNIOR. What's a critic?

ETHEL. They had to give away free popcorn just to get the kids to sit through it.

JUNIOR. It wasn't free. They had to put a deposit on the box.

ETHEL. I have two chances of winning an argument with you. Slim and none. (*She moves to her desk, sits.* CARMEL McGREGOR, *a harried young, aspiring screen-writer in her late teens,* ENTERS DOWN LEFT. *She carries an armload of scripts. There are pencils sticking out of her hairstyle.* ETHEL *busies herself with paperwork*)

CARMEL. (*Crosses to table*) I have the rewrites here, Mr. Dover, Junior. (JUNIOR *sits on one end of the table, takes a script*) I work night and day. I never leave the office.

ETHEL. Isn't that against the rules of the Writers Guild?

CARMEL. I'm not a member. I won't be a member until I get a screen credit.

JUNIOR. (*Brotherly*) That's why you must give me a script I can film. Only then will your name be part of the motion picture industry. (*The tempting bait*) Only then will Carmel McGregor be able to join the Writers Guild.

CARMEL. My dream, my life's ambition.

JUNIOR. I know you appreciate the chance I'm giving you.

CARMEL. Oh, I do, I do.

JUNIOR. I need that *perfect* script. I'm counting on you, Carmel McGregor. The Writers Guild is counting on you. (*With great feeling*) America is counting on you.

CARMEL. I'm trying, Mr. Dover, Junior. I've already given you sixteen versions of this disaster script.

JUNIOR. Perhaps you'll get it right on the seventeenth.

CARMEL. But, Mr. Dover, Junior, you haven't even read this latest draft.

JUNIOR. I don't doubt there's a scene I can use. Few lines of dialog, perhaps. Next time give it a horror slant.

ETHEL. That should be easy.

CARMEL. Mr. Dover, Junior, you said you never wanted anything to do with another horror story after the failure of ZOMBIES OF THE STRATOSPHERE.

JUNIOR. It was not a failure. It was ahead of its time.

ETHEL. What about the one that preceded it—CURSE OF THE FISH PEOPLE? I suppose that was ahead of its time, too.

JUNIOR. I'll pretend I didn't hear that.

ETHEL. What about your "Love Story of the Century" —COBRA WOMAN MEETS JESSE JAMES? I suppose that, too, was ahead of its time.

JUNIOR. With our new disaster film all our past, uh, "artistic successes" will be forgotten.

ETHEL. You mean it's going to be that bad?

JUNIOR. It's going to be that *good!* That *great!* That *sensational!* That—

CARMEL. (*Bedazzled*) —EXTRA-SUPER COLOSSAL!!! (GINGER ENTERS)

GINGER. Sylvia Metroland is here.

JUNIOR. (*Stands*) Show her in, show her in. (GINGER EXITS DOWN LEFT)

ETHEL. (*Stands*) What's that newshound want?

JUNIOR. Never turn down publicity. Remember, there are three ways of spreading the news: telephone, telegraph—

ETHEL and CARMEL. Or tell Sylvia Metroland.

JUNIOR. Check. (SYLVIA METROLAND, *Hollywood's leading film reporter, gushes in. Dark glasses, eccentric costume, pad and pencil ready for "items." She wears an odd-looking hat**)

SYLVIA. (*Opens her arms for an embrace*) Junior!

JUNIOR. (*Opens his arms for an embrace*) Sylvia! (*They march across stage, meet* CENTER. *They kiss—or rather they go through the "ritual" of show biz affection —that is, their lips pucker and smack but never meet. Cheek to cheek they face the audience, still puckering and smacking*)

*A good running gag for SYLVIA is her hat. If it can be managed, on each subsequent appearance what appears to be the same hat gets bigger and bigger—like a "live, growing thing." This will necessitate several "versions" of the same hat. If not, assorted ludicrous hats will suffice.

ETHEL. Hello, Sylvia.

JUNIOR. (*A wave to* CARMEL) This, Sylvia, is the greatest writer since William Shakespeare.

SYLVIA. Who?

JUNIOR. Shakespeare. *William* Shakespeare.

SYLVIA. What studio is he with?

JUNIOR. Not important. What is important is that this little lady is writing my next production. (CARMEL *is intimidated by the "presence" of such an illustrious "writer" as* SYLVIA METROLAND)

SYLVIA. What's her name?

CARMEL. (*So nervous she curtsies*) Carmel McGregor, ma'am.

JUNIOR. Run along, Carmel. Write, write, write.

CARMEL. (*Moves* LEFT, *hugging her scripts*) I will, Mr. Dover, Junior. I will. I'm so grateful.

JUNIOR. Don't mention it.

CARMEL. (*Another nervous curtsy to* SYLVIA) Ma'am. (CARMEL EXITS)

SYLVIA. Strange child. (*Brightens*) Tell me everything about this latest project. (SYLVIA *moves to sofa, sits, pencil poised*) You haven't had a hit since SKATE-BOARD MADNESS.

ETHEL. That was A.I.P.

SYLVIA. Hmmmmmm?

ETHEL. American International Pictures. They produced SKATEBOARD MADNESS.

SYLVIA. I thought Junior produced that.

ETHEL. Only sounds like something he'd produce.

JUNIOR. (*Eager to impress* SYLVIA, JUNIOR *crosses to sofa in an expansive mood*) My new film has everything. Earthquakes, famine, rampaging insects, infernos, typhoons, mudslides, savage lobsters, hurricanes— (*Quickly disinterested,* SYLVIA *folds her notepad*)

SYLVIA. (*Matter-of-fact*) No one wants to see another disaster film. They're *passé*. (SYLVIA *pronounces it "pass-E"*)

ETHEL. Couldn't have said it better myself.

JUNIOR. Ah, but, Sylvia, I will have every big name in Hollywood starring in my film.

SYLVIA. That's not possible.

JUNIOR. Don't forget this studio is "Home of the Stars."

SYLVIA. It *was* "Home of the Stars" —when your father was head of the studio. This lot hasn't had a name since Apassionatta Abalone. That was a *long* time ago.

ETHEL. Whatever happened to Apassionatta? Is she dead.

JUNIOR. Only partially. (*Drops to one knee*) Have faith, Sylvia. Faith. (*Gestures wildly*) Look at that marquee out there. See what it says?

SYLVIA. (*Stares over heads of audience*) I'm not wearing my reading glasses.

JUNIOR. It says —"JUNIOR DOVER, JUNIOR, PRESENTS A DOVER'S EXTRA-SUPER COLOSSAL FILMS, INC. PRODUCTION. STARRING Bronco Whinny—"

SYLVIA. Bronco Whinny!

JUNIOR. "—Flint Wormwood—"

SYLVIA. Flint Wormwood!

JUNIOR. "—Gee-Gee Fontaine, Bob Everlove, Chuckles Lafoon, Theo Bartok—" (*As* JUNIOR *excitedly mentions a name* SYLVIA *repeats it in awe, until—*)

SYLVIA. (*Stands, annoyed*) I'm not as big a fool as I used to be.

ETHEL. Been on a diet?

SYLVIA. No one could get all those names. Gee-Gee Fontaine doesn't even speak to producers.

ETHEL. Smart woman.

JUNIOR. Whose side are you on? I tell you, Sylvia, when you mix stars and disaster you get *"Magic Time."*

SYLVIA. Film like that would cost twenty million dollars. Maybe even a small fortune.

JUNIOR. (*Stands, snaps his fingers*) I already have the financing. (*Crosses back to table*)

SYLVIA. (*Still not convinced*) What do you call this film?

JUNIOR. What else—DISASTERAMA!!!

ETHEL and SYLVIA. DISASTERAMA! (GINGER Enters Down Left)

GINGER. Chuckles Lafoon.

JUNIOR. Who? (CHUCKLES *pushes her way in front of* GINGER)

CHUCKLES. Who! Chuckles Lafoon, funniest lady in show business, that's who! Which one of your two heads am I talking to? (CHUCKLES *is a wild-looking comedienne. Her trademark is outlandish garb, the crazier the better. Her hair looks as if a windstorm dressed it. When she tells one of her terrible hoary jokes, she immediately follows it with her own raucous laugh. She clutches a script under her arm*)

JUNIOR. Chuckles, baby!

CHUCKLES. When I was sitting outside I heard someone mention "diet." I should be so lucky. I used to be so skinny I had to put a coat hanger in my mouth lengthwise so I wouldn't float down the shower drain. Ha, ha, ha! (*No one else laughs. Suddenly,* CHUCKLES *looks fierce, taps script, addresses* JUNIOR *with a threatening tone*) Maybe you don't want me to star in your new flick? (*Instantly,* JUNIOR *gets the message, starts to laugh*)

JUNIOR. What a great gag that was! Ha, ha, ha. Wasn't that a great gag, Ethel?

ETHEL. Ha, ha, ha! (*She stops as abruptly as she began*)

JUNIOR. Wasn't that a knee-slapper, Sylvia?

SYLVIA. Ha, ha, ha. (*She stops.* SYLVIA *gives* GINGER *a frosty look*)

CHUCKLES. What's the matter with her? (JUNIOR *motions her to laugh*)

GINGER. (*Feebly*) Ha, ha, ha. (CHUCKLES *gestures for* GINGER *to laugh louder . . . longer. She turns to the others like a musical conductor, encouraging them to laugh. Soon* GINGER, JUNIOR, ETHEL *and* SYLVIA *are carrying on like hyenas*)

CHUCKLES. All right, that's enough! (*They continue to laugh*) *Cease!* (*Silence*) That's what the world needs more of. Laughter. From the heart.

GINGER. I think I heard that coat hanger gag on Dial-A-Joke. (JUNIOR *and* ETHEL *go into shock*)

CHUCKLES. Listen, kid, you're only young once and if you work it right once is enough. Get out of here. (GINGER *flees.* SYLVIA *moves in with pad and pencil*)

SYLVIA. It's true, then? You are going to be in Junior's new film? (JUNIOR *goes behind table*)

JUNIOR. She's going to *star* in it! (CHUCKLES *crosses to table,* SYLVIA *behind her, taking everything down.* ETHEL *moves to* UPSTAGE *end of sofa*)

CHUCKLES. Great script, Junior. One hundred and thirty pages of pure gold.

JUNIOR. And you're in one hundred and twenty-eight of them.

CHUCKLES. I want to talk to you about that. Those other two pages stink. (JUNIOR *reaches around table, takes her script*)

JUNIOR. Easily fixed. (*He rips two pages from the script*) Happy?

CHUCKLES. I'm going to enjoy working for you. How do you like my new dress? A parachute company down in San Diego whipped it up for me.

JUNIOR. (*Thinking she'll enjoy the gag*) What did they whip it up with—an eggbeater? (JUNIOR *laughs.* ETHEL *and* SYLVIA *join in.* CHUCKLES *looks dangerous*)

CHUCKLES. *Cease!* (*Silence*) We better get one thing straight. As long as I'm on this film there's only going to be one joker in the deck. Me. (*Building in intensity*) Me! (*Practically raving*) *Me! Me! Me! Chuckles Lafoon, funniest lady in show business!!!* (*The outburst has drained her of energy, she grabs the table for support, head bowed*)

SYLVIA. (*Applauding*) Wonderful, wonderful, Chuckles. You're going to be great. (JUNIOR *and* ETHEL *applaud.* CHUCKLES *snaps out of it, returns to her zany self*)

CHUCKLES. I'm glad you like the threads, Junior. This outfit I'm wearing brings out the best in me. I always say a girl should use what Mother Nature gave her before Father Time takes it away. Ha, ha, ha! (SYLVIA, JUNIOR, ETHEL, *on cue, join in, laughing away.* GINGER *returns*)

GINGER. He's here!

ETHEL. Who?

GINGER. Bronco Whinny.

JUNIOR. Send him in. (GINGER EXITS)

SYLVIA. (*Excitedly writing away*) You have got the stars! What a story!

ETHEL. I see it happening, but I don't believe it.

CHUCKLES. Bronco Whinny's been on the range so long they ought to call him Dusty. Ha, ha, ha. (BRONCO ENTERS DOWN LEFT. *His costume is "cowboy caricature"—ten gallon hat, high heel boots, fringe dripping from his jacket, enormous belt buckle, holstered pistols hugging his hips. Spurs the size of tin cans. If possible, he should also wear great furry chaps. He carries a guitar slung on his back. Under his arm is tucked a script. His conversation is nearly always a string of western cliches*)

BRONCO. I jus' come in off the trail. Mah hoss hankerin' fer a taste of hay . . . bury me not on the lone prairie . . . I run a tight corral . . . git along l'il doggie . . . my foot in the stirrup and hand on the horn, I'm the best cowboy star that ever was born.

ETHEL. Oh, brother.

SYLVIA. (*Notebook ready*) Some comments for your fans, Bronco?

BRONCO. Nope.

SYLVIA. Nope?

BRONCO. Bronco Whinny is a coyote of few words.

ETHEL. If that were only true.

CHUCKLES. When there's nothing more to say, Bronco Whinny is still saying it. Ha, ha, ha!

BRONCO. I take my western image serious, Chuckles.

CHUCKLES. No offense, pony boy. Hope you're not going to sing in this picture.

BRONCO. I am. My fans expect it. Y' know, I developed my singin' voice in the bathtub.

CHUCKLES. Maybe you ought to take more baths. Ha, ha, ha. (BRONCO *frowns. Plainly he and* CHUCKLES *are not going to hit it off*)

BRONCO. Ma'am, if I warn't a gentleman I'd say somethin'.

CHUCKLES. If I "warn't" a lady, I'd listen. Ha, ha, ha. (*Again,* BRONCO *frowns. Storm clouds are gathering on his brow. He strides to the table and only now do we realize he's* terribly *bowlegged. His spurs "clank-clank" as he moves*)

BRONCO. This hyar script, Junior, I had my dialogue

rewritten for my "unique western personality." Ain't easy to capture the essence of Bronco Whinny on paper.

JUNIOR. (*Takes, flips the pages*) Let's see . . . (*Reads*) "Nope . . . yup . . . nope . . . yup . . . nope . . . yup . . ."

ETHEL. That's all he's going to say?

SYLVIA. No one in Hollywood today can say "Nope" and "Yup" the way Bronco Whinny can.

BRONCO. Yup.

JUNIOR. Whatever you say, Bronco. I like your new dialogue. It's, uh, it's, uh—

ETHEL. Original.

JUNIOR. That's the word I was looking for. Original.

BRONCO. Much obliged.

CHUCKLES. Come on, Bronco, lunch is on me—just throw a tablecloth over my face. Ha, ha, ha!

BRONCO. I don't eat lunch. Whenever I'm hungry I chaw on a piece of rawhide. (BRONCO EXITS DOWN RIGHT —"*clank, clank, clank*")

CHUCKLES. If he's got a brain he ought to let it go to his head. Ha, ha, ha! (*Imitating* BRONCO's *bowlegged gait*, CHUCKLES *pretends to hitch up a gun holster and* EXITS *after* BRONCO) Nope . . . yup . . . nope . . . yup . . . nope (*She's out*)

SYLVIA. Imagine Bronco Whinny and Chuckles Lafoon together in the same film!

ETHEL. I can't imagine.

SYLVIA. It'll be on my weekly television show. *Ciao.* (*She* EXITS DOWN LEFT, *overjoyed with her scoop*)

ETHEL. Chuckles and Bronco will be at each other's throat first day on the set. You've almost convinced me there *is* going to be a film.

JUNIOR. It's in the bag.

ETHEL. So long as we don't get caught holding it. (GINGER SCREAMS *from* OFFSTAGE) What on earth? (GINGER SCREAMS *again, runs in*) Ginger! What is it! (*She stops only long enough to point* DOWN LEFT, *screams, runs off* DOWN RIGHT. ETHEL *and* JUNIOR *tense, exchange a worried look. An "apparition" appears* DOWN LEFT—*garbled in a floor length dark gown. Very theatrical, out-of-date . Long gloves. On the head sits a turban.*

The face is coated in white powder, the lips painted black, the mascara eyes bulge—haunted-looking. She carries a "trade" paper)

JUNIOR. (*Stage whisper to* ETHEL) It's Apassionatta Abalone.

ETHEL. (*Amazed*) She is alive. (APASSIONATTA *points an accusing finger at* JUNIOR)

APASSIONATTA. *Ingrate!* (JUNIOR *looks behind him*)

JUNIOR. Where?

APASSIONATTA. You're the ingrate, Junior!

JUNIOR. What have I done? (APASSIONATTA *twitches* CENTER. *Where her "career" is concerned, she's threatening and regal*)

APASSIONATTA. (*Holds up paper*) It's here in *Daily Variety*. You're casting a new film with the biggest stars in Hollywood.

ETHEL. Junior won't deny that.

APASSIONATTA. Then why haven't you cast the biggest star of all?

ETHEL. Who's that?

APASSIONATTA. (*A fierce look at* ETHEL) Who else— *Apassionatta Abalone!*

JUNIOR. You?

APASSIONATTA. I'm not aware there's more than one Apassionatta Abalone. (ETHEL *gets the chair from her desk, moves it to the visitor*)

ETHEL. Won't you sit down. This is a treat meeting you. My grandfather had pictures of Apassionatta Abalone all over the house.

APASSIONATTA. So do I. (*She sits*)

JUNIOR. (*A "compliment"*) You were a star before I was born.

APASSIONATTA. *Everything* was before you were born.

JUNIOR. What I'm trying to say is—film-making has changed. A lot has happened in Hollywood since the fifties when you last appeared in anything. Maybe you don't remember the fifties.

APASSIONATTA. I remember the fifties. There was nineteen fifty-one, nineteen fifty-three, uh, nineteen fifty-seven, uh—

JUNIOR. This picture is modern. Nothing old-fashioned about it.

APASSIONATTA. Are you trying to say there's something old-fashioned about me?

JUNIOR. No, that is, I mean—your style of acting was popular. (*Pause*) Some time back.

APASSIONATTA. (*She is furious, she doesn't so much stand as erupt*) Don't talk down to me, you pimple. I made this studio! Who will ever forget Apassionatta Abalone in JUNGLE GARDENIA, LIPSTICK AND LOVE, QUEEN OF THE WILD SCHNAUZERS? (APASSIONATTA *strikes a dramatic pose with her head*) Look at this face. The face of a star. The face of Apassionatta Abalone. All other actresses and actors have faces like pudding.

JUNIOR. I'll tell you what. Maybe I could use you as one of the dress extras in the party scene. (APASSIONATTA, *shocked, grabs* ETHEL's *arm, fearful she might faint*)

APASSIONATTA. Extra!

JUNIOR. You'll have to supply your own gown.

APASSIONATTA. Extra!

JUNIOR. Maybe I can get some publicity mileage out of it. "Old-time actress returns."

APASSIONATTA. Apassionatta Abalone doesn't have to "return." Apassionatta Abalone never left Hollywood. I'll tell you what left—*intelligence!* (*She strides* DOWN LEFT, *turns*) I hope you'll come to your senses. I hope I'll see you again.

JUNIOR. (*Waves*) Let me know the visiting hours. (APASSIONATTA *fixes him with a glacial glare,* EXITS *with flamboyant style*)

APASSIONATTA. Idiot. (*She's out.* ETHEL *takes a step after her*)

ETHEL. Like a page from the past.

JUNIOR. Walking history. After her career started to go down the tube, any picture with Apassionatta Abalone in it was a guaranteed bankruptcy. (GINGER, *cautious, sticks her head in* DOWN RIGHT)

GINGER. Is it safe?

ETHEL. Perfectly.

GINGER. Whoever that was, she should rattle before she strikes. They're here.

JUNIOR. Who?

GINGER. Weren't you expecting someone from the Bumble Bank of Burbank? (JUNIOR *comes from behind his desk*) They're on their way in. (*Nods* DOWN RIGHT)

JUNIOR. I'll buzz if I want you. (GINGER EXITS DOWN LEFT. JUNIOR *stands beside* ETHEL) We're on our way. Fame and fortune!

ETHEL. If you could bottle enthusiasm you'd be a millionaire tonight. (*He turns* RIGHT, *throws open his arms*)

JUNIOR. Welcome, Mr. Bumble, welcome! (MRS. BUMBLE ENTERS. *She's a commanding society matron. Her only weakness is her obsession to put her daughter in films. In this respect* MRS. BUMBLE *is the classic "stage mother"*)

MRS. BUMBLE. I came in my husband's place. I trust it will be all right.

JUNIOR. Did you bring his checkbook?

MRS. BUMBLE. I beg your pardon?

ETHEL. Junior was making a little joke.

MRS. BUMBLE. In this town everyone has to be a comedian. (*Obviously,* MRS. BUMBLE *is no slouch when it comes to the Hollywood scene*)

ETHEL. (*Indicates sofa*) Won't you sit down. (MRS. BUMBLE *crosses to sofa, sits.* ETHEL *pushes her desk chair back in position.* JUNIOR *steps toward sofa*)

MRS. BUMBLE. I don't believe in wasting time. Your studio already owes the bank a considerable sum.

JUNIOR. A temporary condition.

MRS. BUMBLE. Unless you turn a profit on your next film, I will own this studio.

JUNIOR. Gulp.

MRS. BUMBLE. My husband has left the decision of whether or not to advance the money entirely to me. (*Like some mad comedian in a silent film,* JUNIOR *drops to one knee and slavishly kisses her bejeweled fingers. She pulls her hand away, stands*) Stop that at once. I have every·intention of advancing the money.

JUNIOR. ·You do! (*He jumps to his feet*)

MRS. BUMBLE. On one condition.

ETHEL. What condition?

MRS. BUMBLE. You must star my baby daughter.

JUNIOR. I didn't know you had a baby daughter.

MRS. BUMBLE. Baby Bernice will be a sensation!

ETHEL and JUNIOR. (*Incredulous*) Baby Bernice?

MRS. BUMBLE. Come in, Baby Bernice, precious. Show the gentleman your talent! (BABY BERNICE *leaps in from* DOWN RIGHT *and hits the stage with a thud*)

BABY BERNICE. *Hi!* (BABY BERNICE *is clearly in her teens. Dressed absurdly, far too young for her age in an attempt to maintain the "baby" image. She's like a walking Kewpie doll—incredible blonde hair or yellow hair. Curly. She walks with all the grace of a reasonably intelligent chimp. For a final touch she carries a large stuffed Panda or Teddy Bear*)

MRS. BUMBLE. Isn't she something?

ETHEL. (*Droll*) She certainly is.

MRS. BUMBLE. She sings and dances! Perform, Baby Bernice, perform! (MRS. BUMBLE *sits again on the sofa,* ETHEL *and* JUNIOR *move to the table and stare in wonderment—and horror.* BABY BERNICE, *truly an obnoxious child, takes* CENTER, *sings*)

ANYTHING CAN HAPPEN
("Meet Me In St. Louis, Louis")

BABY BERNICE.
ANYTHING CAN HAPPEN, TRULY
ANYTHING AT ALL
IF YOU ONLY KEEP ON SMILING
SUMMER, SPRING AND FALL.

IF YOU'LL ONLY STAY WITH LAUGHTER
LUCK WILL BE FOREVER AFTER.
REMEMBER
ANYTHING CAN HAPPEN, TRULY
ANYTHING AT ALL.

(*This is followed by a brief, wretched tap dance*)

MRS. BUMBLE. (*Applauding*) That was wonderful, Baby Bernice. Wonderful! Wasn't she wonderful?

JUNIOR. She has a certain, uh, "something."

MRS. BUMBLE. (*Stands*) You know talent when you see it.

ETHEL. Mrs. Bumble, the days of child stars are in the past. The public doesn't want to see children in starring roles.

MRS. BUMBLE. Perhaps I didn't make myself clear. Either this picture stars Baby Bernice Bumble, or there is no picture.

BABY BERNICE. If I can't be a movie star, I'll hold my breath 'til my head gets fat! (*She puffs out her cheeks, holds her breath, her eyes rolling*)

MRS. BUMBLE. You are endangering the life of that child.

JUNIOR. Make her stop!

MRS. BUMBLE. Well, Junior, do we sign a contract, or do we go home? (BABY BERNICE *is puffing—her cheeks about to burst, her eyes about to pop.* JUNIOR *crosses to her*)

JUNIOR. Baby, I'm going to make you a star. (JUNIOR *whacks her on the back. With hissing sound of escaping breath,* BABY BERNICE *exhales, holds out an arm in a gesture for applause.* BLACKOUT. CURTAIN. *A moment of blackness, then* SPOTLIGHT *hits* DOWN LEFT, *pinpointing a* TELEVISION ANNOUNCER)

ANNOUNCER. . . . and now Channel Twenty-nine, Hollywood's direct line to the stars, presents filmland's most celebrated columnist. First a word from our sponsor—*Los Angeles Fizz*, the only soda pop west of the Mississippi that comes complete with its own burp. Favorite of Hollywood greats. In two bottle sizes: stupendous and gigantic. Remember, whenever you think of Sylvia Metroland, think burp. (*He belches*) Now Channel Twenty-nine, Hollywood's direct line to the stars, presents—*Sylvia Metroland!* (*He applauds enthusiastically,* EXITS DOWN LEFT *as his spot dies.* SPOTLIGHT *hits* DOWN RIGHT *to reveal* SYLVIA *with a wide phony smile on her face. In one hand she holds papers containing "news items." In the other—a hand bell. She rings it four times slowly, never allowing the smile to crack*)

SYLVIA. Another Sylvia Metroland report from Glittertown, U.S.A. . . . . there is absolutely no truth to the rumor that Lassie is contemplating a divorce. For this outrageous slur I award the perpetrator my lowest rating. One bell. (*She rings the bell once, checks another "item"*) Magnanimous Studios was turned down yesterday in its bid to purchase the film rights to *Webster's Seventh New Collegiate Dictionary*. Pity. It was a best-seller, too. For Magnanimous' effort to return significance to the screen I awarded three bells. (*She rings the bell three times, checks another "item"*) There's *thrilling* news coming from producer Junior Dover, Junior. He's readying a new film titled DISASTERAMA and he's lining up every *big* name in Glittertown. I don't know how he manages it, but there's no stopping him. For courage, fortitude and vision, I award Junior Dover, Junior, my highest rating. Four bells. (*She rings the bell, smile never fading. One, two, three, four, five. On the fifth ring,* SYLVIA *looks most unhappy, realizing she's goofed*)

BLACKOUT

ACT ONE

SCENE 2

JUNIOR's *office. Few days later.*
GINGER *is behind the table, viewing some costume sketches,* ETHEL *is in front, stacking scripts.*

GINGER. I do like this design. Gee-Gee Fontaine will look lovely in it.
ETHEL. She might. If she signs a contract.
GINGER. Mr. Dover, Junior, tells everyone she's going to be in the picture.
ETHEL. That doesn't mean it's true. In this town when you're ninety-nine percent sure, you've got a fifty-fifty chance. (TELEPHONE RINGS. ETHEL CROSSES *to her desk, picks it up on the* THIRD *go*) This is a recording. You have reached the executive offices of "Dover's Extra-Super Colossal Films, Inc., Home of the Stars, et cetera,

et cetera." (WINIFRED LUNG, *head of the studio's "talent school,"* ENTERS DOWN LEFT. *She's an English type, rather grand, fluttery*)

WINIFRED. I don't know what I'm expected to do with that miserable child. She'll never be a star!

GINGER. (*Fascinated by the various costume designs*) Who's that, Miss Lung?

WINIFRED. Who else would it be? The only one enrolled in the studio's talent school. Baby Bernice Bumble.

GINGER. I heard Mr. Dover, Junior, say if anyone could do anything with her, you could.

WINIFRED. I could drown her like a cat.

GINGER. I'd better get back to work. This place has certainly sprung to life.

WINIFRED. Baby Bernice Bumble in "Disasterama." (*Grimaces*) It's grotesque. (GINGER *starts to* EXIT DOWN LEFT)

GINGER. Leave everything to Mr. Dover, Junior. (*She's* OUT)

WINIFRED. That's what he'd like me to do. My purse, my checkbook, my savings bonds. (ETHEL *finishes at desk, puts down receiver, moves to* WINIFRED)

ETHEL. What's the problem, Winifred?

WINIFRED. Baby Bernice should be in quarantine, not in talent school. She's at least fourteen, maybe older. You can't fool the public.

ETHEL. Mrs. Bumble says Baby Bernice is pressing ten.

WINIFRED. "Baby" Bernice has been pressing ten for so long it's pleated. To think that I, Winifred Lung, the finest dramatic teacher in films, has been reduced to coaching a pupil who couldn't get top billing in a flea circus.

ETHEL. We're counting on you.

WINIFRED. I'm only staying on for one reason.

ETHEL. Loyalty.

WINIFRED. No, I haven't built up enough points for Social Security retirement benefits. (*She moves* DOWN LEFT, *turns*) When that happens, Winifred Lung fades into the sunset like the end of a Bronco Whinny film.

(*She does an imitation of a horse's neigh,* ETHEL. *Exits.* JUNIOR *hurries* IN DOWN RIGHT)

ETHEL. Where have you been?

JUNIOR. Busy, busy, busy.

ETHEL. So is the telephone. Every agent in town is calling. The trade papers want to know who you're signing for director.

JUNIOR. Who else—Plato Voltaire.

ETHEL. (*Shocked*) Plato Voltaire! The hack from television? You can't be serious. "Disasterama" is a multi-million-dollar epic. Whenever he does a show, the ratings are so low they can't even measure them.

JUNIOR. I want to see him the minute he arrives.

ETHEL. He arrived an hour ago. I tried to get rid of him, but he wouldn't leave. (JUNIOR *goes behind the table, sits.* ETHEL *steps to desk, presses intercom*) Send in Mr. Voltaire. You'd better have a talk with Winifred Lung.

JUNIOR. She's lucky she's got a job. I only keep her on because she was such a good friend of my father's.

ETHEL. Not to mention the fact she rents you a room. Cheap. (PLATO VOLTAIRE *ENTERS DOWN LEFT wearing a beret and carrying a walking stick or riding crop. There's a script under his arm. He's vain, arrogant, talentless, convinced he's a genius*)

JUNIOR. Voltaire, baby! (VOLTAIRE *takes the script, spits on it*)

VOLTAIRE. Phooey! This script is garbage! Throw it in the incinerator! I spit on it. (*He does*) I spit on it again. (*He does.* ETHEL *sighs, folds her arms, leans against her desk*)

JUNIOR. I have a fantasy you don't like the script.

VOLTAIRE. You expect Plato Voltaire to work on this mockery? A director of my talent? My genius? My reputation?

ETHEL. Your reputation!

VOLTAIRE. (*Bristles*) What's the matter with my reputation?

ETHEL. The woman who marries you will be canceled in thirteen weeks.

VOLTAIRE. Malicious gossip.

ETHEL. The television networks refer to you as "Kiss of Death Voltaire."

VOLTAIRE. I am no longer welcome at the television networks because of professional jealousy.

JUNIOR. This is your big chance to get out of television and into feature films.

VOLTAIRE. Not with this script.

JUNIOR. Voltaire, I shall overcome all your objections.

VOLTAIRE. (*Haughty*) With what?

JUNIOR. Money. (VOLTAIRE *is impressed, flips a few pages of the script*)

VOLTAIRE. Perhaps I could do a re-write. Give the script the famous "Voltaire touch." (JUNIOR *comes from behind the desk, puts his arm around* VOLTAIRE's *shoulder*)

JUNIOR. Rewrite the whole thing from top to bottom if you want. We'll give you the screen credit.

VOLTAIRE. (*Checks script*) What about this name— Carmel MacGregor?

JUNIOR. (*Takes script, tosses it over his shoulder*) Forget her. We'll give her a credit for additional dialogue.

VOLTAIRE. I can see it now—"Disasterama," a film by Plato Voltaire, directed by Plato Voltaire, written by Plato Voltaire.

ETHEL. Why don't you take the leading role?

VOLTAIRE. Yes, yes, I can see that, too. "Plato Voltaire starring in Disasterama!" (*Modestly*) No, I'm afraid not. People might think I'm egotistical. (GINGER *runs* IN *from* DOWN LEFT)

GINGER. She's here!

ETHEL. Who?

GINGER. (*Jumping up and down in glee*) Gee-Gee Fontaine!

ETHEL. Your leading lady, Voltaire.

VOLTAIRE. I must meet her at once.

JUNIOR. No, no, you let me handle Gee-Gee.

VOLTAIRE. (*Shrugs*) Whatever you think best. (JUNIOR *motions him to* EXIT DOWN RIGHT. *He* CROSSES) I hope you appreciate the honor I'm doing you. (*Enraptured*) A film by Plato Voltaire, directed by Plato Voltaire, written by Plato Voltaire. (*He stops, kisses the back of his hand several times*) You genius, you. (*He* EXITS *as a*

MAID, *carrying a large jewel chest overflowing with gems,*
ENTERS DOWN LEFT. *Maybe a uniformed* CHAUFFEUR.
They stand at attention)
    GEE-GEE'S SERVANT(S). (*An announcement of great
importance*) *Miz Gee-Gee Fontaine!* (GEE-GEE *totters in
on high platform shoes—a living Hollywood legend,
gorgeous, eye-filling, radiant, larger than life. Stunning
hair, preferably blonde or platinum. Even though it's
the middle of the day, she wears a floor-length gown
and there's a fur draped over her shoulders. Jewels
are everywhere on her person: arms, fingers, neck,
ears, etc. She's D-A-Z-Z-L-I-N-G. Her dialogue sounds
as if it has been painstakingly rehearsed. She's not terribly bright. One important thing about* GEE-GEE—*when
she speaks, she sounds like a squeaking mouse. Consult*
PRODUCTION NOTES. GINGER EXITS)
    JUNIOR. Gee, Gee-Gee, it's great to greet ya! (*He
charges toward her, ready for a kiss and an embrace*)
    GEE-GEE. (*One hand up to stop him*) Stop! (JUNIOR
skids to a halt) I don't kiss.
    JUNIOR. Whatever you say.
    GEE-GEE. However, as is my custom, when I am
pleased with some artistic endeavor, I award baubles.
(*She looks into the jewelry chest, plucks out some cufflinks*) Diamond cufflinks in appreciation for that wonderful script you sent to me. It will be an honor to star in
your new film.
    JUNIOR. Gee, Gee-Gee, I don't know what to say.
    ETHEL. You might offer her a seat.
    JUNIOR. Please sit down, Gee-Gee.
    GEE-GEE. I'll try. (*Because* GEE-GEE *is so tightly cos-
tumed, it's difficult for her to walk. She hobbles to sofa
as best she can, turns and very slowly eases herself down
—fearful that if she moves too fast, the dress will split.
She makes it, smiles*)
    JUNIOR. I'm glad you liked the script.
    GEE-GEE. One hundred and thirty pages of dramatic
intensity and I'm in one hundred and twenty-eight.
Every star in Hollywood supporting me in teeny-weeny
bit parts.
    ETHEL. Am I hearing right?

GRETA. (OFFSTAGE, DOWN LEFT) Don't bother to announce me. Doors don't mean a thing to Greta Gutt. (GINGER *backs* IN, *trying to hold off the toughest agent in town*—GRETA GUTT. *Tweedy, aggressive, business-sharp*)

GINGER. You can't push in this way.

GRETA. I'm doing it.

GINGER. I'm sorry, Mr. Dover, Junior.

ETHEL. Don't worry about it, Ginger.

JUNIOR. (*Arms wide*) Greta, baby! (*She brushes by him on the way to the table. Under her arm she carries what looks like a window shade.* GINGER EXITS)

GRETA. Let's get down to business. My time is money. (*She puts down the "window shade"*) I represent the biggest stars in Hollywood. I'm the best agent in town. I know it. The public knows it.

GEE-GEE. You don't represent me and I'm a big star.

GRETA. You'd be even bigger if they didn't have to dub your voice.

GEE-GEE. There's nothing the matter with my voice. (ALL *look at* GEE-GEE *in wonder. Is it possible she doesn't realize what she sounds like?*)

GRETA. You want Bob Everlove, "The Boy Next Door," and Flint Wormwood and his .357 Magnum?

ETHEL. He wants.

GRETA. Okay, you got 'em.

JUNIOR. Great!

GRETA. On my terms.

ETHEL. Which are? (GRETA *throws open the "window shade," which isn't a window shade at all. It's a contract*)

GRETA. (*Machine gun delivery*) Junior, all you have to do is sign on the bottom line. I want forty percent of gross, exclusive subsidiary rights, paperback serialization, no default clause written into the contract, a penalty charge on postponement of starting date. Also, right to approve any and all publicity stills—

ETHEL. Those are impossible demands. No producer would sign.

JUNIOR. I'll sign. (*With that,* JUNIOR CROSSES *to contract.* GRETA *takes out a pen*)

GRETA. Another million-dollar deal engineered by Greta Gutt, Hollywood's top agent. (*To* JUNIOR, *indi-*

cates) Sign here. There. And there. (JUNIOR *signs*) Bob Everlove is outside. I'll give him the good news. You'll never regret this, Junior. Smartest move you ever made.

GEE-GEE. Is Flint Wormwood outside, too?

GRETA. (CROSSES DOWN LEFT *with contract*) Naw. He's at the shooting gallery on Santa Monica pier. Has to keep in training. (*She* EXITS. GEE-GEE *staggers to her feet. If* SERVANT(S) *are used, they assist*)

GEE-GEE. I don't want to meet Bob Everlove yet. It's bad luck to see a bit player before the start of a film.

JUNIOR. (*Motions* DOWN RIGHT) Go out this way. (*She totters* RIGHT)

GEE-GEE. (*Trying to remember what she's memorized for the occasion*) This will be a monumental achievement in the history of film making.

JUNIOR. Gee, Gee-Gee, thanks again for the links.

GEE-GEE. Likewise. (*Struggling to maintain her ballance,* GEE-GEE *totters* OFF DOWN RIGHT)

ETHEL. What did she mean—she's in one hundred and twenty-eight pages of the script? She means Chuckles, doesn't she?

JUNIOR. What a stroke of luck. Young America's heart-throb—Bob Everlove.

ETHEL. (*Unimpressed*) It's a tossup as to who's more conceited. Voltaire or your new "star." Every time "The Boy Next Door" passes a mirror, he takes a bow. (*On cue,* BOB EVERLOVE *bounces in. He wears a tennis outfit. All white. He carries a racquet and his toothy smile looks like it's been pasted on*)

BOB. (*Waves racquet*) Tennis, anyone?

JUNIOR. (*Arms wide*) Bob, baby. (JUNIOR *moves to embrace him.* BOB *holds him back by sticking the tennis racquet in his belly*)

BOB. (*Snarls*) Not too close, Mr. Producer. I just had my hair sprayed.

JUNIOR. Bob, baby, did Greta Gutt give you the good news?

BOB. Good news for you. There's not a producer in town who wouldn't give an arm and a leg to have "The Boy Next Door" in his lousy movie.

ETHEL. Knowing producers as I do—it would be some-one else's arm and leg.

JUNIOR. Did you read the script?

BOB. Who needs scripts? It's *me* the public wants. Look at this face. It's money in the bank. (*Turning his head as he rants on in self-love*) Left profile. Right profile. Three-quarter profile. (*A note of triumph*) Full face!

JUNIOR. (*Applauding*) Every young woman in America will be at your feet.

ETHEL. If they're scrubwomen.

BOB. You scratch my back, Junior, and I scratch yours.

ETHEL. It's Junior's palm that's itchy, not his back. (BOB *steps* DOWN LEFT, *calls* OFFSTAGE)

BOB. Come in, ladies. (SALLY *and* PAULINE ENTER. *They're young movie enthusiasts, awed by the Hollywood "mystique" but determined to make good*) This is Sally and this is Pauline.

JUNIOR. Any friend of Bob Everlove is a friend of Junior Dover, Junior. (*With his "public"* BOB EVERLOVE *is all wholesome charm and consideration*)

BOB. Sit over here, girls. Be comfortable. (*He guides them to the sofa*)

PAULINE. Thank you, Mr. Everlove. (SALLY *and* PAULINE *sit*)

BOB. Let's get rid of that "Mister" Everlove. I want you to think of me as "Bob, the boy next door." (SALLY *and* PAULINE *sigh romantically*)

ETHEL. (*Sotto*) Yeech.

BOB. Junior, old pal, old buddy, *amigo*.

ETHEL. (*To* JUNIOR) Hold onto your wallet.

BOB. Not only are Sally and Pauline among my greatest fans—they're co-presidents of my international fan club.

SALLY. A million members in twenty-three foreign countries.

BOB. Plus the good ole U.S. of A. (*Grins boyishly*) I'm going to ask you a favor, neighbor.

ETHEL. Remember what I said about your wallet.

JUNIOR. So ask.

BOB. Pauline and Sally want to learn the film business.

JUNIOR. There's a camera shop down the street.

BOB. I meant the *movie* film business.

ETHEL. Junior was afraid that was what you meant.

SALLY. Pauline and I know all about projectors, lens, editing and sound.

PAULINE. We won two prizes in high school for documentaries.

SALLY. And we've written a script.

JUNIOR *No scripts!*

BOB. (*Smiles*) Excuse me a moment, please.

SALLY. Of course, Mister Ever— (*Corrects herself*) Bob. (*Still smiling,* BOB CROSSES *to* JUNIOR, *the racquet in his grip like a club. He takes* JUNIOR *by the arm and moves* DOWN RIGHT)

BOB. Guess I didn't make myself clear. (*With that, he jabs* JUNIOR *with the racquet*) Sally and Pauline represent my fans. My public. (*Another jab*) If "The Boy Next Door" isn't happy, you're going to be very glum, Junior. (*Another jab*) Get me?

JUNIOR. (*Rubbing his belly*) Ow. (*Forces a smile*) Gotcha.

BOB. (*Grins, slaps* JUNIOR *on the back*) That's great, neighbor. (*Turns*) All right, girls, you're in the movie business. (*Delighted,* SALLY *and* PAULINE *jump up*)

SALLY. Thank you, Bob.

BOB. Don't mention it. It's the least I could do.

PAULINE. No wonder your fans love you.

BOB. I don't want to hear one more word of gratitude. Let's go out on the lawn. The sun's still good. I imagine you'll want to snap some pictures of me. (*He strides* DOWN LEFT, *a jaunty wave of the tennis racquet to* JUNIOR) See you later, neighbor. (*He's* OUT. SALLY *and* PAULINE *follow, overjoyed*)

SALLY. Isn't he wonderful!

PAULINE. He's not a star—he's a saint! (*They're* OUT. ETHEL *moves* DOWNSTAGE, *looks* LEFT)

ETHEL. He could be "The Boy Next Door"—*if* the boy next door is a slightly sadistic fathead. (*She turns, sees* JUNIOR *rubbing his belly*)

JUNIOR. He packs a mean tennis racquet.

ETHEL. The things you put up with to make your movie. Is it worth it?

JUNIOR. *Anything's* worth it.

ETHEL. How are you going to get away with it? I don't

mean the money. You've got that, thanks to Mrs. Bumble. Every star you've signed seems to think he or she is the whole picture and everyone else is in a supporting role.

JUNIOR. You noticed, huh?

ETHEL. No evasions. The truth.

JUNIOR. (*Eases into it*) I don't have Carmel MacGregor doing rewrites. I have her doing a new script each time. One script is tailored for Chuckles Lafoon, the next for Gee-Gee Fontaine, the next for Theo Bartok—

ETHEL. —You mean each star has a *different* script!

JUNIOR. Check.

ETHEL. Which script are you going to film?

JUNIOR. All.

ETHEL. All! I'd better call the hospital. You're suffering a breakdown. (*She moves to her desk*)

JUNIOR. I'll film all the scripts so no one will get wise.

ETHEL. You'll have twenty hours of film!

JUNIOR. I'll edit it all down to about two.

ETHEL. What happens when they find out what you've done?

JUNIOR. They won't find out until it's too late. By then, the picture will be on its way, a success.

ETHEL. Aren't you forgetting your main attraction— Baby Bernice Bumble. Your stars aren't going to stand still for a *baby* in the film. She might steal too many scenes.

JUNIOR. (*Snaps his fingers as an idea strikes*) I've got it!

ETHEL. It's called insanity.

JUNIOR. Those kids "The Boy Next Door" brought in. They want to learn the film business. I'll let them work with Baby Bernice. That'll keep her out of my hair. (*As JUNIOR speaks, sure of his plan, a claw-like hand grips the side of the advertising/dressing screen*) Why do you think I hired a pinhead like Plato Voltaire? Another director would catch on in a minute, but not him. (*Stealthily, like a panther about to pounce, from behind the screen appears the malevolent shape of* APASSIONATTA ABALONE. *Smile of victory on her museum face*)

ETHEL. If one word of this got out—

JUNIOR. Only two people know. You and me.

APASSIONATTA. *And Apassionatta Abalone!!!* (JUNIOR *and* ETHEL *give a cry of alarm, hug each other like Hansel and Gretel might have done in the presence of evil*) Deceiver! Cheat! Fraud! (*She lurches forward to* RIGHT *of* JUNIOR *and* ETHEL) I could ruin you!

ETHEL. (*Nervously*) We didn't know you were hiding back there.

APASSIONATTA. *That* is obvious. With a single breath I could *destroy* you, Junior.

JUNIOR. If you'd only let me explain.

APASSIONATTA. *Don't interrupt!* (JUNIOR *winces, clings to* ETHEL *for support*) Explanations are useless. I heard it all.

JUNIOR. Tell you what I'll do—

APASSIONATTA. I'll tell *you* what *you'll* do. You'll announce that Apassionatta Abalone is returning to the screen. That she has graciously consented to star in your new film.

JUNIOR. Impossible—

APASSIONATTA. Where a great talent like mine is concerned, *nothing* is impossible! If you don't do this, I shall inform each of the "lesser talents" how you plan to deceive them.

ETHEL. You can't. You wouldn't.

APASSIONATTA. I can and I will. Don't get any funny ideas about cutting me out of the film. I'll be watching you like a hawk.

ETHEL. More like a vulture.

APASSIONATTA. I'm waiting for your answer.

JUNIOR. (*Desperate*) Who knows? It might work. After all— (*To* ETHEL) this is Hollywood.

ETHEL. Anything can happen.

JUNIOR. Okay, Apassionatta. You win.

APASSIONATTA. Wise decision. (*With great dramatic flair*) Light the lights, get ready to record, move the cameras in close. (*Sweeping gesture*) *A star is re-born!*

CURTAIN

END OF ACT ONE

ACT TWO

SCENE 1

When LIGHTS COME UP, *we discover* MAP SELLER DOWN RIGHT *in front of curtain. He or she has a "sandwich board" with the lettering:* MAPS TO THE STARS' HOMES. *In one hand he holds maps, waving them at unseen passing motorists.*

MAP SELLER. Maps to the stars' homes! Maps to the stars' homes! Only a dollar a map. See where the stars live and play! See them on their lawns, see them taking out the trash, see them walking the dog! Maps to the stars' homes! Etc. (*As the* MAP SELLER *repeats the spiel, voice trailing off, a* TOURIST GUIDE ENTERS DOWN LEFT *with several* TOURISTS *dressed gaudily in sunglasses, funny hats, shorts, etc. Cameras around their necks*)

TOURIST GUIDE. (*Indicates curtain*) . . . and here we are at the fabulous studios of Dover's Extra-Super Colossal Films, Inc. —Home of the Stars! (TOURISTS *"oooooh" and "aaaaah," snap pictures*) Behind these monumental walls resides a world of magic and fantasy, denied ordinary mortals. (*More "oooooh" and "aaaaah"*) You are, indeed, fortunate people to be standing out here on the sidewalk thinking about getting in. For behind the gates of this fabled empire the greatest film of all time is in production—DISASTERAMA!!! (*More "oooooh" and "aaaaah"*) We will now proceed to the studio cafeteria where we will have lunch with the stars! (*Biggest "oooooh" and "aaaaah"*) Actually, we won't have lunch *with* the stars. (*A great moan goes up from the* TOURISTS) However— (*A greater sigh of hopeful expectation*) We will be able to stand *outside* the studio cafeteria *on* the terrace, *at* the window, and *peer in!* (*A tumultuous* AD

LIB *of glee, followed by applause, etc.*) This way to the cafeteria window! (*He crosses* DOWN RIGHT *and out.* TOURISTS, *excited, follow.* MAP SELLER *yells out to unseen motorists*)

MAP SELLER. . . . see them on their lawns, see them taking out the trash, see them walking the dog! Without a map you wouldn't be able to tell real tinsel from phony tinsel! Maps to the stars' homes! Etc. (*He follows the* TOURISTS, *his voice continuing the pitch for a map sale. Curtain opens to reveal a sound stage.* CONSULT PRODUC- TION NOTES. *Three small tables with chairs have been placed* CENTER, *one* UPSTAGE *somewhat, one* LEFT, *one* RIGHT. *The tables represent a setting that will be used in a film sequence. Supposedly we're in a ship's "salon." To enhance this effect some potted palms or plants can be added. Maybe an easy-to-strike scenery flat with a port- hole, etc. Outside this "inner set,"* EXTREME DOWN RIGHT, *is a dressing table and chair for* GEE-GEE. *There's a standing camera* DOWN RIGHT *pointed at the "salon," a director's chair* DOWN LEFT. *Alongside* STAGE LEFT *there's a makeup table with a bench.* GEE-GEE *is seated at her table.* CAMERA OPERATOR *is focusing. The "A.D." or* AS- SISTANT DIRECTOR *is standing in the "salon"*)

ASSISTANT DIRECTOR. (*Frantic*) Where is Flint Wormwood?

CAMERA OPERATOR. The second unit had to use him in some re-takes.

ASSISTANT DIRECTOR. Why doesn't anyone tell me these things? Where's his standin?

CAMERA OPERATOR. Mister Voltaire fired the standin this morning.

ASSISTANT DIRECTOR. Why?

CAMERA OPERATOR. He asked a question.

ASSISTANT DIRECTOR. How am I supposed to frame this shot without Flint Wormwood or his standin? Miz Fontaine can't do it alone.

GEE-GEE. Yes, she can, Mister Assistant Director. We don't need Flint Wormwood or his standin. I'm more than enough. (*She walks to* ASSISTANT DIRECTOR)

ASSISTANT DIRECTOR. We're filming this ship sequence

in a few minutes. If the shot isn't right, Mister Voltaire will fire *me!*

GEE-GEE. (*The "professional"*) Less talk, more action.

ASSISTANT DIRECTOR. You're right. (*Wipes forehead*) I've never worked on a picture like this. I hope I never do again.

GEE-GEE. Where do I stand?

ASSISTANT DIRECTOR. Right here, dear. (GEE-GEE *positions herself*) Now bend back. (*She does*) Flint Wormwood will hold you in a mad embrace. Bend back more. (GEE-GEE *is in a most awkward position. She bends back more*)

GEE-GEE. (*Can barely talk*) How's this?

ASSISTANT DIRECTOR. (*To* CAMERA OPERATOR) How's it look? (CAMERA OPERATOR *looks through camera*)

CAMERA OPERATOR. Yeah, I'll be able to get a good shot. Only—

ASSISTANT DIRECTOR. Only what?

CAMERA OPERATOR. Can she bend back a bit more?

ASSISTANT DIRECTOR. Little more, Miz Fontaine. (GEE-GEE *is about to crack in sections, manages to bend back an inch or two more, softly groaning, uncomfortable*)

CAMERA OPERATOR. That's good. Mark it. (ASSISTANT DIRECTOR *marks the position with a piece of chalk*)

ASSISTANT DIRECTOR. Let's check the overhead cameras. Mister Voltaire wants to use some trick angles. (ASSISTANT DIRECTOR *and* CAMERA OPERATOR EXIT RIGHT. *They've forgotten* GEE-GEE *who remains in the middle of the "salon" like a petrified human pretzel*)

GEE-GEE. Help. (*Pause*) Anybody out there? (*Another pause*) I think I'm going to snap in two. (FLINT WORMWOOD, *a ruggedly handsome star who specializes in tough cop roles, dressed impeccably like an F.B.I. agent, or I.B.M. junior executive,* ENTERS LEFT)

FLINT. Sorry I'm late. Those re-takes took longer than I thought.

GEE-GEE. Could you help me up, Flint. Please.

FLINT. (*Looks around*) Where's the crew?

GEE-GEE. (*Desperate*) I'm going to fall over. Hurry.

FLINT. Y'know, Gee-Gee, I don't understand the plot of this film.

GEE-GEE. What's a plot? (GEE-GEE *collapses on the floor with a groan. Flint barely takes notice.* GEE-GEE *picks herself up.* FLINT *opens his jacket to display a shoulder holster and weapon*)

FLINT. I'm out of ammunition.

GEE-GEE. I could have hurt myself. Why didn't you help me?

FLINT. (*Plucks at his trousers*) And ruin my crease?

GEE-GEE (*Annoyed*) You're no gentleman. (FLINT *takes out the revolver, blows on the muzzle as if it were smoking, affects a "mean" pose*)

FLINT. I never was. Flint Wormwood is 100% rogue male. Tough, rugged, macho, honcho. Flint Wormwood is raw meat.

GEE-GEE. Baloney. (*She slaps him in the face. He reacts like a small boy*)

FLINT. I'm telling Greta Gutt what you did. She'll fix you. You wait and see! (EXITS LEFT, *calling out*) Greta! Greta! Gee-Gee Fontaine hit me! (APASSIONATTA ENTERS DOWN RIGHT *in front of dressing table*)

APASSIONATTA. I'm ready for my closeup.

GEE-GEE. Mister Voltaire says the only way to photograph you in a closeup is through a horse blanket.

APASSIONATTA. (*Moves to* GEE-GEE) Tell me, Miz Fontaine, have you always had that . . . uh, *voice?*

GEE-GEE. When I first came to Hollywood and they told me they would have to dub my voice, I was upset.

APASSIONATTA. Understandable.

GEE-GEE. I was so upset, I was housebroken. But, when one is as gorgeous as me what does a voice matter?

APASSIONATTA. True. You have courage and you're bold.

GEE-GEE. (*Plucks at her hair*) Who's bold? I got hair.

APASSIONATTA. Did I hear the vocal mannerisms of Flint Wormwood, my leading man?

GEE-GEE. He's my leading man.

APASSIONATTA. Nonsense. Haven't you read the script?

GEE-GEE. No.

APASSIONATTA. Unfortunately, he can't play a love scene. I'll have to teach him.

GEE-GEE. Don't be gross. You're old enough to be his

grandmother's mother. (APASSIONATTA's *face is a mask of subdued rage. She forces a smile*)

APASSIONATTA. Let's not quarrel. I've brought you a gift.

GEE-GEE. I like gifts. (APASSIONATTA *takes an apple and holds it out like the witch tempting Snow White. She is unimpressed*) That looks like an apple.

APASSIONATTA. Aren't you observant. (*Offers*) Go on. Take a bite.

GEE-GEE. This reminds me of a fairy tale I read.

APASSIONATTA. *You* read.

GEE-GEE. Well, someone read it to me. Snow White and the Seven Dwarfs.

APASSIONATTA. (*Haughty*) In your case they would be seven drips.

GEE-GEE. Is that an insult?

APASSIONATTA. (*Crosses to* DOWN RIGHT *table*) You're dumber than I thought if you think it's a compliment. I'm warning you. Keep your hands off Flint. He's mine!

GEE-GEE. Mine.

APASSIONATTA. Silly actress, to believe that Flint Wormwood could be interested in you or that the great Apassionatta Abalone would stoop so low as to poison an apple. I laugh at the suggestion. (*Slow, false*) Ha . . . ha. (APASSIONATTA *takes a bite from the apple, puts it on dressing table*, EXITS DOWN RIGHT)

GEE-GEE. Anyone would think you're the star of this picture. There's only one star here and I'm it . . . her . . . she . . . (*Still struggling for the right pronoun* GEE-GEE EXITS *as* MRS. BUMBLE *and* BABY BERNICE ENTER UP LEFT *and into "salon"*)

MRS. BUMBLE. This is where they'll be filming next. So exciting.

BABY BERNICE. I'm not in this scene. I don't understand why I'm never in any of the scenes with my supporting players.

MRS. BUMBLE. Junior wants you to have *special* attention. After all, you're the lead in this picture. He's counting on you.

BABY BERNICE. If you ask me there's something fishy going on.

MRS. BUMBLE. It's probably the tuna you had for lunch.

BABY BERNICE. I want to be in the next scene. If I can't be in the next scene I'll hold my breath 'til my eyes pop and my lips turn purple, and my kneecaps peel. (*Repeats* "breath bit," *her cheeks puffed out like an expanding balloon*)

MRS. BUMBLE. Baby Bernice, stop that! Stop! Oh, help, somebody! Help! (*In a panic,* MRS. BUMBLE *starts to* EXIT DOWN LEFT, *but is stopped by the appearance of that great horror star,* THEO BARTOK. *He's dressed in sombre colors and wearing a flowing cape. His skin is the color of chalk, his lips thin and red. A walking vampire!* MRS. BUMBLE *screams, recovers*) Oh, it's you, Mister Bartok.

THEO. (*Voice like a whisper in a tomb*) Naturally. Who else would dress like this?

MRS. BUMBLE. Baby Bernice is being difficult again. I don't know what to do. (THEO *crosses to* BABY BERNICE, MRS. BUMBLE *with him*)

THEO. Stop holding your breath. Bad for digestion. (BABY BERNICE *shakes her head*) Stop, I say, or I'll bite you on the neck. (BABY BERNICE *refuses. Hand out like* Dracula) Obey me!

MRS. BUMBLE. You're so forceful. Exactly as you are in your horror movies. Listen to the nice vampire, Baby Bernice. (*No good.* THEO *kicks her in the rump*)

BABY BERNICE. Aw! I hate you! I'll get even for what you did! No one kicks Baby Bernice and gets away with it.

MRS. BUMBLE. Baby Bernice, behave. She's so temperamental. A true artist. (*Furious, rubbing her backside,* BABY BERNICE *goes to makeup table, sits*) I'm delighted you're in this film.

THEO. This film is the pits. Theo Bartok redeems it by his presence. I only do these films for the money. My true love is the theatre. Only this morning I was offered the role of Shylock in *The Merchant of Venice*.

MRS. BUMBLE. A star of your stature must be careful.

THEO. What do you mean?

MRS. BUMBLE. Tell them if you can't have the role of

the merchant you won't be in the play. (*From* DOWN LEFT *the raucous* LAUGHTER *of* CHUCKLES LAFOON—*"Ha. Ha. Ha"*)

CHUCKLES. (ENTERS) This studio would make a great fire.

THEO. I can't stand that clown. (BRONCO ENTERS *behind* CHUCKLES)

CHUCKLES. I heard that, tall, dark and gruesome.

THEO. I am happy to say I have no romantic scenes with you.

CHUCKLES. What's the matter with me?

THEO. If you must know—you're vulgar.

CHUCKLES. Making a living biting people in the neck isn't my idea of a class act.

THEO. I wouldn't get close to you with a ten foot pole.

CHUCKLES. How about a six foot Italian? Ha, ha, ha.

BRONCO. Howdy, Mrs. Bumble.

CHUCKLES. (*Crosses*) Tell me, is it true?

MRS. BUMBLE. Is what true?

CHUCKLES. You're so rich you have alligator bags under your eyes. Ha, ha, ha.

BRONCO. Chuckles, I hope you don't live to be as old as your jokes.

CHUCKLES. Watch it, saddle sore. There's only one star making the funnies around here. Me!

BABY BERNICE. (*Beating her hands on the makeup table*) I hate you! I hate you all! (*All look* LEFT)

CHUCKLES. What's eating the kid?

MRS. BUMBLE. Artistic temperament.

THEO. If she doesn't learn to relax she might get ulcers.

CHUCKLES. Kid like that doesn't get ulcers. She gives 'em. Ha, ha, ha. (BOB EVERLOVE *bounces in* DOWN RIGHT, *tennis racquet in hand, still dressed in white*)

BOB. Hi, ho, gang.

CHUCKLES. (*Sizing up his outfit*) What happened to you? Did you fall in a tub of vanilla ice cream? Ha, ha, ha. (THEO, MRS. BUMBLE *and* BRONCO *join in the laughter*)

BOB. I could learn to loathe you, Chuckles.

BABY BERNICE. I loathe you all! I hate you, I hate you!

THEO. One big happy family.

BOB. (*Leans on dressing table*) I've never had such a supporting cast.

ACTORS. *Supporting cast!*

BOB. (*As his hand touches something unpleasant*) Auuuuugh!

OTHERS.
What's wrong?
What happened?
Etc.

BOB. (*Holds it up*) This apple.

CHUCKLES. So?

BOB. There's teeth in it. A set of dentures.

CHUCKLES. Someone lost their choppers? Let's have Junior do a remake of JAWS. We'll call it GUMS. Ha, ha, ha. (BOB *moves to others.* APASSIONATTA *unseen, sneaks in* DOWN RIGHT, *a hand covering her toothless mouth. She grabs the apple from the table,* EXITS *surreptitiously*)

BOB. I'm going to protest to the Screen Actors Guild. As star of this film, I deserve respect. I don't get anything around here but abuse.

THEO. Who says you're the star? I'm the star!

CHUCKLES. I'm the star!

MRS. BUMBLE. Baby Bernice is the star!

BRONCO. Nope. I am.

AD LIBS. I am! I am! Etc. (*Blowing a whistle,* VOLTAIRE ENTERS UP RIGHT *followed by* SCRIPT PERSON, ASSISTANT DIRECTOR, CAMERA OPERATOR. *A* MAKEUP ARTIST ENTERS UP LEFT, *goes to makeup table*)

VOLTAIRE. Please, please, order on the set. I must have quiet.

ASSISTANT DIRECTOR. Quiet!

SCRIPT PERSON. Quiet on the set!

CAMERA OPERATOR. Quiet! (VOLTAIRE *sits in director's chair,* SCRIPT PERSON *beside him.* CAMERA OPERATOR *goes behind camera,* ASSISTANT DIRECTOR *beside him*)

VOLTAIRE. Take your places for the giant iceberg sequence.

ASSISTANT DIRECTOR. Places!

SCRIPT PERSON. Places for the giant iceberg sequence!

CAMERA OPERATOR. Places! (THEO EXITS UP RIGHT.

CHUCKLES, BRONCO, BOB *take places at tables as best fits the stage picture.* GEE-GEE, FLINT *and* APASSIONATTA ENTER, *sit at tables,* MRS. BUMBLE *goes to* BABY BERNICE)

VOLTAIRE. Makeup for Miz Abalone!

SCRIPT PERSON. Makeup!

ASSISTANT DIRECTOR. Makeup for Miz Abalone!

CAMERA OPERATOR. Makeup! (MAKEUP ARTIST *crosses to* APASSIONATTA *with ·a large puff heavy with powder, slaps actress in the face, returns to table.* APASSIONATTA *chokes.* DIALOGUE *through business*)

VOLTAIRE. Remember, children, this has been a harrowing voyage. The ship has been attacked by a giant squid, the bottom has been eaten through by an insane killer shark, you have made your way through a howling typhoon and a three mile high wave. Typhus has broken out among the passengers, and now, to break the monotony, you are being pursued by a revenge-seeking iceberg. Oh, this is going to be *so good!* What reviews I'm going to get. (*Kisses his hand*) Genius, you.

BRONCO. Question.

VOLTAIRE. What is it, Bronchitis? I mean Bronco.

BRONCO. I fergit my first line.

VOLTAIRE. Script!

ASSISTANT DIRECTOR. Script!

CAMERA OPERATOR. Script! (SCRIPT PERSON *goes to* BRONCO *with script, hands it to him. He stares at the page for several seconds*)

BRONCO. What's this hyar script written in? Chinese? (SCRIPT PERSON *turns it around. He's been looking at it upside down. He studies the page*) I got it now.

CHUCKLES. I bet in high school you had underwater marks. Everything below C-level. Ha, ha, ha. (*Others join in.* BRONCO *fumes.* SCRIPT PERSON *returns to place*)

VOLTAIRE. Attention, children, attention. I have positioned wide-angle lens and sound equipment everywhere. On the ceiling . . . off-right . . . off-left . . . in the floorboards. (*As he names each position,* CAST *looks— something like spectators at a ping-pong match*)

ASSISTANT DIRECTOR. Better hurry up, Mister Voltaire.

VOLTAIRE. Plato Voltaire doesn't "hurry up." Plato Voltaire can't be rushed. Plato Voltaire takes his time.

ASSISTANT DIRECTOR. Union's called a sympathy strike with the sanitation workers. We've got ten minutes.

VOLTAIRE. We'd better hurry up. Lights!

SCRIPT PERSON. Lights!

CAMERA OPERATOR. (STAGE LIGHTING *concentrates on "inner set," the "salon." Fringe areas go dim.* ASSISTANT DIRECTOR *steps in front of camera with clapboard*)

ASSISTANT DIRECTOR. DISASTERAMA—*Scene 104— Take 14.* (BABY BERNICE *strides to* CENTER *of salon*)

BABY BERNICE. (*Arms akimbo*) I want to sing and dance.

VOLTAIRE. Not now, little girl.

BABY BERNICE. I want to be in this scene.

VOLTAIRE. Later.

BABY BERNICE. (*Demands*) I said I want to be in this scene and I want to sing.

MRS BUMBLE. Isn't she adorable?

BABY BUMBLE. If I don't sing, my mother will tell my father to take all his money out of this production.

ALL. *Sing, Baby Bernice, sing!* (*Instantly,* BABY BERNICE *becomes all cuddly warmth and innocence, smiles happily.* CAMERA OPERATOR *"films" as she sings*)

BABY BERNICE.

ANYTHING CAN HAPPEN, TRULY
ANYTHING AT ALL
ETC.

(*As* BABY BERNICE *nears the end of her musical "entertainment,"* MAKEUP ARTIST *crosses to her and slaps her in the face with the powder-laden puff. Applause from* CAST *as song ends.* MAKEUP ARTIST *returns to position*)

ASSISTANT DIRECTOR. Three minutes, Mister Voltaire.

VOLTAIRE. Here we go, everyone. Magic time! (ASSISTANT DIRECTOR *steps in front of camera.* BABY BERNICE *staggers, half-blinded by the powder, for a seat at one of the tables*)

ASSISTANT DIRECTOR. DISASTERAMA—*Scene 104— Take 15.* (*Slaps clapboard, returns to position*)

VOLTAIRE. *Sound!*

ASSISTANT DIRECTOR. *Sound!*

SCRIPT PERSON. *Sound!* (SOUND EFFECTS OF WIND, RAIN, GALE, ETC. —*to approximate a storm*)

VOLTAIRE. *Action!* (PASSENGERS *rock back and forth for several moments to suggest a rolling ship*)

GEE-GEE. What new terror on the high seas awaits us?

APASSIONATTA. (*The ham, arms lifted to heaven*) We are doomed, doomed!

BRONCO. Yup.

BOB. I'll never sail on this line again. (THEO ENTERS UP RIGHT, *still wearing his vampire cape, but he's added a Captain's hat*)

THEO. Ladies and gentlemen, an important announcement. (*All freeze*) The ship is sinking. (GENERAL AD LIB *of shock. Screams, etc.*)

AD. LIB.
Sinking! Doomed! We're doomed!
I want my mama!
Do something!
Etc.

THEO. However— (*Again,* PASSENGERS *freeze*) I wouldn't worry about it. Everything's under control. It's the meteorite I'm concerned about.

ACTORS. Meteorite!

THEO. Yes, it's about to hit the ship.

GEE-GEE. When?

THEO. (*Checks watch*) Now. (SOUND OF BOOM!!! STAGE LIGHTS FLASH!!! PASSENGERS *yell, stumble onto the salon floor in one great pile of arms and legs*)

VOLTAIRE. *Cut! Print it!*

BLACKOUT

CURTAIN

ACT TWO

SCENE 2

LIGHTS UP ON CURTAIN. TOURIST GUIDE ENTERS DOWN RIGHT, *followed by* TOURISTS, *some reading maps, others snapping pix, etc.*

TOURIST GUIDE. Come along, come along. More to do and see. (*Stops* CENTER) Did you enjoy lunch?

TOURISTS. Mmmmmm. Delicious.

TOURIST GUIDE. We will next visit the Stars' Gift Galaxy, where all proceeds are donated to the Albanian Actors' Home. You will be able to purchase garments and other accessories worn by actual stars in actual pictures. (*"Ooooooh," "aaaaah"*) Gee-Gee Fontaine's foot pads, the gut from Bob Everlove's tennis racquet, fertilizer from Bronco Whinny's working ranch, and personally autographed photos of the stars! (*Big "oooooah," big "aaaaah"*) Personally autographed by the star's personal secretary. (*Big sigh of disappointment*) After that, we'll visit the Filmland Museum to view Burt Reynolds' pickled tonsils. (*Biggest "oooooah," "aaaaah" yet*) Stay close. Don't get lost. (TOURIST GUIDE *moves* DOWN LEFT)

TOURIST. (*Calling after* GUIDE) Is there anyplace we can buy a jar of smog? (*As they trail off,* LIGHTS DIM. SPOTLIGHT *hits* DOWN RIGHT. TELEVISION ANNOUNCER ENTERS, *addresses homeviewers*)

ANNOUNCER. . . . and now Channel Twenty-nine, Hollywood's direct line to the stars, presents filmland's most celebrated columnist. First a word from our new sponsor, Miranda Anti-Itch Lotion. Friends, itching is a curse. With Miranda Anti-Itch Lotion needless embarrassment is over. Simply empty the bottle on the itch and Miranda Anti-Itch Lotion will do the scratching for you, thus freeing your hands for more serious labor. (*Quickly, matter-of-fact*) Apply Miranda Sealing Wax in case Miranda Anti-Itch Lotion breaks the skin. (*Enthusiastic*) And now Channel Twenty-nine, Hollywood's direct line to the stars, presents—*Sylvia Metroland!* (*He applauds, doesn't leave stage.* SPOTLIGHT *hits* DOWN LEFT *as* SYLVIA ENTERS)

SYLVIA. Another Sylvia Metroland report from Glittertown, U.S.A. . . . Absolutely no truth to the rumor that Universal Studios is preparing to remake the Rudolph Valentino classic THE SHEIK starring the King of Saudi Arabia. One bell for this false alarm. (*Rings bell once*) Good news from producer Leonard Rose. He's planning to film the Dead Sea Scrolls. (*Grins*) I didn't even know they were ill. Three bells for producer Rose. (*Rings three*

times) The really exciting news continues to be the filming of Junior Dover, Junior's blockbuster—DISAS-
TERAMA. The entire country is waiting for its release.
Will it be the classic disaster film of all time as Junior
predicts? For returning suspense to Glittertown, I award
Junior Dover, Junior, my highest award. Four bells.
(*Rings bell—once, twice, three times. Pause, making cer-
tain she doesn't make another mistake. Relieved, she
rings the fourth bell, smiles.* ANNOUNCER *takes a bell
from behind his back and rings it for the "fifth" sound.*
SYLVIA *looks devastated, shoots him a dirty look.* LIGHTS
OUT)

    (CURTAIN OPENS *to reveal a room in the Writers'
    Building.* CARMEL, *like an overworked clerk in a
    Charles Dickens' novel, sits on a stool,* CENTER, *be-
    hind a high desk or table. Scripts are stacked every-
    where and wastebaskets are overflowing with
    crumpled paper. Food containers litter the area.*
    CARMEL *types away furiously, like a soul possessed.
    Stops, reads what she's created*)

    CARMEL. Exterior—Southern mansion—day—establish-
ing shot. Cousin Amanda comes running up the steps to
greet her Uncle Cornpone. She's crying. (*Disgusted with
her efforts, she rips the page from the the typewriter,
crumples it, tosses it over her shoulder*) Cousin Amanda
must have read the script. (WINIFRED ENTERS DOWN
RIGHT, *followed by* SALLY *and* PAULINE)
    WINIFRED. Where's Junior?
    CARMEL. How should I know? I'm only the slave.
    WINIFRED. The young ladies want to show Junior some
rushes.
    CARMEL. Rushes of Baby Bernice Bumble?
    WINIFRED. I think I've made some improvement with
her voice. She no longer sings as if she gargled with old
razor blades.
    SALLY. Ethel said he was headed this way.
    CARMEL. Maybe he'll show, maybe he won't. You never
know with Junior.
    WINIFRED. I must say you've changed.

CARMEL. Have I?

WINIFRED. Definitely. You used to be so self-effacing.

CARMEL. Exhaustion and no pay take their toll.

PAULINE. No pay?

WINIFRED. You mean Junior doesn't pay you a salary?

CARMEL. He says since he doesn't ask me for a salary, it isn't fair of me to ask him for one.

WINIFRED. Outrageous! That young man obviously believes in the Eleventh Commandment.

SALLY. What's that?

WINIFRED. Thou shalt not be found out. My advice to you, Carmel, is stand up for your rights. Don't allow Junior to push you around.

PAULINE. If he'd only look at what we've done with Baby Bernice.

SALLY. It would prove how good we are.

CARMEL. If I see him, I'll tell him.

WINIFRED. Nothing to accomplish here. Back to the set. (*She* EXITS DOWN RIGHT)

SALLY. Baby Bernice Bumble needs us.

PAULINE. We need her. (*As they* EXIT, FLINT WORM-WOOD *hurries in, looking over his shoulder, fearful*)

FLINT. Okay if I hide in here?

CARMEL. Mister Wormwood, this is a pleasure. I've been working on a new script for you. Let's see. It must be here somewhere. (*She starts to search, scripts falling to the floor*)

FLINT. Later. I gotta hide. (*With that, he ducks by the desk, out of sight*)

CARMEL. Mister Wormwood, what's wrong?

FLINT. Ssssssh. (*From* OFF STAGE *the regal voice of—*)

APASSIONATTA. (OFF STAGE) Flint. Flint, darling, where are you hiding?

FLINT. Don't tell her I'm here. (APASSIONATTA *sweeps in* LEFT)

APASSIONATTA. Where is he?

CARMEL. Miz Abalone, this is a pleasure. I've been working on a new script for you. (*Searches*) It must be here somewhere.

APASSIONATTA. Where have you hidden my leading man?

CARMEL. I haven't hidden anyone. (FLINT *attempts to escape by crawling* RIGHT *on hands and knees*)

APASSIONATTA. Stop! (FLINT *freezes*) He's shy in my presence. Too much beauty and talent does that to a man.

FLINT. (*Gets up*) Thanks for the compliment.

APASSIONATTA. I was referring to *my* beauty and *my* talent. Flint, we must rehearse our love scene.

FLINT. (*Anxious to avoid the "scene"*) We can't do it now. Mister Voltaire's busy.

APASSIONATTA. Who needs that toad? *I'll* rehearse you.

FLINT. Do we have to?

APASSIONATTA. Practice makes perfect.

FLINT. I don't know my lines.

APASSIONATTA Who needs lines?

CARMEL. I think I have a script right here. (*More frantic searching*)

APASSIONATTA. We won't need dialogue. My gestures convey more than mere words ever could. (CROSSES *to* FLINT) Take me in your arms.

FLINT. I shouldn't do love scenes. My fans don't like it.

APASSIONATTA. I said—take me in your arms. (CARMEL *watches, fascinated.* FLINT *awkwardly takes Apassionatta in his arms*) Now, I breathe heavy. (*She does*) My eyes become dazed. (*They do*) My heart beats like a drum. Boom, boom, boom.

FLINT. I play tough cops, Apassionatta. I don't have love stuff in my scripts.

APASSIONATTA. This will be a breakthrough for you. I'm planning to use you in my next film. A romantic saga. I'll play Cleopatra and you'll play Lafitte the pirate.

FLINT. I think Greta Gutt is calling me. I'd better go. (*It's obvious* FLINT *is terrified by this relic from another era*)

CARMEL. I don't hear anyone.

APASSIONATTA. Your heart is beating like a drum, too.

FLINT. It is?

APASSIONATTA. You look at me and your eyes breathe fire.

FLINT. How can eyes breathe fire? (*Disgusted,* APASSIONATTA *breaks the embrace*)

APASSIONATTA. You're not trying! You can have it either way, Flint. I can be a great boost to your career, or I can smash it. I have Junior Dover, Junior's ear.

FLINT. (*Worried*) What does she mean? His ear?

CARMEL. He listens to her.

APASSIONATTA. If I say cut this person from a scene, he's out. You could be the face on the cutting room floor.

FLINT. (*Moves to* CARMEL, *nervous*) I think she's sprung a leak. She's bananas.

CARMEL. Maybe you'd better humor her.

FLINT. You're right. I've seen cases like her before.

CARMEL. Where?

FLINT. The wax museum.

APASSIONATTA. I'm waiting.

FLINT. I think I'm supposed to do this scene with Gee-Gee Fontaine.

APASSIONATTA. Forget Gee-Gee Fontaine. She's a nobody.

FLINT. I can't rehearse in somebody's office. It's unnatural.

APASSIONATTA. I understand. The mood is all wrong. No problem. (*With a grand wave of her hand, she turns* DOWN RIGHT) Encore! (*A* MUSICIAN ENTERS, *preferably a violinist. He takes position* DOWN RIGHT, *begins to play some romantic melody.* FLINT *and* CARMEL *are amazed*) We repeat the love scene.

FLINT. I was afraid of that.

APASSIONATTA. If music be the food of love, play on! (MUSICIAN *plays a bit faster, then returns to the syrupy "melody"*) Let the melody sink into your bloodstream. Feel it to the ends of your toes. (FLINT *lifts his shoe, touches the tip*)

CARMEL. Gosh, Miz Abalone. It's like the old days. When films were beginning.

APASSIONATTA. Take me in your arms, fool.

FLINT. She calling me a fool?

CARMEL. It's old-style acting. All the vamps called their boyfriends fools. You'd better do as she says.

FLINT. I'll do it, but I won't like it.

CARMEL. Amour, Flint, amour. (*Reluctantly,* FLINT

takes her in his arms, the MUSIC *supplying a ludicrously mushy background*)

APASSIONATTA. I breathe heavy. (*She does, in a parody of all the great love scenes from silent films*) My eyes become dazed. (*Does something with her eyes*) My heart beats like a drum. Boom, boom, boom. (*She pats her heart in rhythm*) Your heart is beating like a drum, too.

FLINT and CARMEL. Boom, boom, boom.

APASSIONATTA. You look at me and your eyes breathe fire.

FLINT. I'll try. (*His attempt to have his eyes "breathe fire" is comical. If possible, he crosses them*)

APASSIONATTA. Your chest pants. (*He breathes heavily, audibly*) Now, the moment audiences have been waiting for. You kiss me.

FLINT. (*Horrified*) *What!*

APASSIONATTA. My eyes closed, I await the kiss.

FLINT. I'd rather kiss a halibut.

APASSIONATTA. What are you waiting for? Kiss me! (*An idea strikes! One arm holds* APASSIONATTA, *while* FLINT *sticks two fingers in his mouth to wet them. He draws them slowly across* APASSIONATTA's *lips*) Oh, Flint, that's what I call a kiss. (FLINT *senses the time is right for escape. He leaves* APASSIONATTA *with her eyes closed,* EXITS RIGHT, *fast.* MUSICIAN *stops playing,* EXITS. ETHEL ENTERS LEFT, *sees* APASSIONATTA *bent back, eyes closed*)

ETHEL. She's doing yoga?

CARMEL. He left, Miz Abalone.

APASSIONATTA. (*Eyes open, straightens up*) Left?

CARMEL. A second ago.

APASSIONATTA. I imagine the intensity of the scene was too much for him. He'll get over it. Which way did he go?

CARMEL. (*Points* RIGHT) That way.

APASSIONATTA. Miz Kent, I think it would be a good idea if Junior dismissed all the other performers. This picture only needs two stars. Myself and Flint Wormwood.

ETHEL. I'll tell him you said so. (APASSIONATTA EXITS RIGHT, *dramatic flourish*)

APASSIONATTA. I'm ready for another closeup, Mister Voltaire! (*She's out*)

CARMEL. Wow! Isn't she something. It's amazing she can still walk. (CARMEL *has managed to get her hands tangled in her typewriter ribbon*) Look at this mess. I must use up a ribbon a day.

ETHEL. Isn't Junior here?

CARMEL. Everyone's looking for him. (*Indicates food containers*) Have some pastry? A Danish, piece of crumb cake?

ETHEL. (*Pokes through a box on top of desk*) Is this the sort of thing you live on?

CARMEL. I have a friend who works in a bakery. If it wasn't for him I'd starve. Go on. Have something.

ETHEL. I'm dieting.

CARMEL. (*Hands her a script*) Here's the new script Mister Dover, Junior, wanted me to write in case he signed that Eskimo star.

ETHEL. (*Takes it*) I doubt if he'll be able to use it. He's close to wrapping up the film.

CARMEL. I'd better wash my hands. (*She* EXITS RIGHT. ETHEL *flips the cover, reads the title*)

ETHEL. *The Frozen Waltz*, original screenplay by Carmel McGregor. (JUNIOR ENTERS DOWN LEFT *in his usual exuberant state*)

JUNIOR. Everything's moving along nicely.

ETHEL. By that I suppose you mean no one's caught on. Incidentally, Sid Rabinowitz called. He's been trying to get you all day.

JUNIOR. I'm renting his theatre for a sneak preview way out in Pomona. Test audience reaction. Top secret. No one except you and me will know about it.

ETHEL. I used to think I'd breathe a sigh of relief when this was all over. Now, I'm not so sure.

JUNIOR. When they see what I've done with the picture, they'll love me. I'll play up to them at the cast party.

ETHEL. You're not going to throw a party?

JUNIOR. Certainly. It's tradition when the film's in the can.

ETHEL. They hate each other. If you get them all together at a party it'll be open warfare.

JUNIOR. You worry too much.

ETHEL. One of us has to.

JUNIOR. Get Rabinowitz on the horn and tell him we're renting his Shanghai Palace for the sneak.

ETHEL. Yes, master. Here's Carmel's new script. (*She hands it to him. He checks title page*)

JUNIOR. *The Frozen Waltz?* That'll never sell. We'll change the title to— (*Thinks*) *The Incredible Melting Dogsled.* How's that?

ETHEL. (EXITS) Rotten.

JUNIOR. (*Calls after her*) That's why I'm a producer and you're a secretary. (CARMEL *returns, drying her hands with a paper towel*) Ah, Carmel, the very lady I wish to see.

CARMEL. I hope you're not going to ask me to write another draft. I'm about written out. (*She moves to desk*)

JUNIOR. (*Gung-ho*) Never be written out. Everything aimed for that great night.

CARMEL. What great night?

JUNIOR. (*Shocked*) What great night? How can you ask? The Academy Awards!

CARMEL. (*Enchanted*) The Academy Awards. (LIGHTS FADE QUICKLY INTO DIMNESS *except for the* FORESTAGE. MUSICAL FANFARE *or* DRUM ROLL. ANNOUNCER ENTERS DOWN RIGHT, *beside him a* YOUNG WOMAN *holding a tray of dolls. She moves* CENTER)

ANNOUNCER. Ladies and gentlemen, honored guests, members of The Academy of Motion Picture Arts and Sciences, a moment you've all been waiting for. Best actress of the year. The nominees are Gee-Gee Fontaine for *Disasterama*, Baby Bernice Bumble for *Disasterama*, Chuckles Lafoon for *Disasterama* and Apassionatta Abalone for *Disasterama*. May I have the envelope, please. (MUSICIAN ENTERS DOWN RIGHT, *hands* ANNOUNCER *envelope*, EXITS. ANNOUNCER *opens, reads*) *The winner is* —Gee-Gee Fontaine, Baby Bernice Bumble, Chuckles Lafoon, Apassionatta Abalone! (*From the wings* LOUD APPLAUSE. *Quickly* GEE-GEE, BABY BERNICE ENTER LEFT; CHUCKLES, APASSIONATTA RIGHT. *Each takes a doll from the tray. They stand in a straight line and address audience*)

ACTRESSES. We want to thank all the little people. Thank you. (*They* EXIT *as* ANNOUNCER *speaks*)

ANNOUNCER. Nominees for best actor. Flint Wormwood for *Disasterama*, Bronco Whinny for *Disasterama*, Theo Bartok for *Disasterama*, Bob Everlove for *Disasterama*. May I have the envelope, please. (*Repeat business*) *The winner is*—Flint Wormwood, Bronco Whinny. Theo Bartok, Bob Everlove! (FLINT, BRONCO ENTER RIGHT, THEO *and* BOB LEFT. *They take dolls, face audience*)

ACTORS. We want to thank all the little people, too. Thanks, little people. (*They* EXIT *as* ANNOUNCER *speaks*)

ANNOUNCER. The nominee for best director is Plato Voltaire for *Disasterama*. Never mind the envelope. The winner is— (*Before* ANNOUNCER *can finish*, VOLTAIRE *runs in, grabs a doll and runs off*)

VOLTAIRE. *Mine! Mine! Mine! It's all mine! You, genius, you!*

ANNOUNCER. The biggest moment of all. Best picture of the year. The nominee is—*Disasterama*. May I have the envelope, please. (MUSICIAN ENTERS, *hands envelope*, EXITS) *The winner is—Disasterama!!!* (APPLAUSE, MUSICAL FANFARE OR DRUM ROLL) Here accepting the Oscar, the producer of *Disasterama*—Junior Dover, Junior! (*More* OFFSTAGE APPLAUSE. JUNIOR *takes doll, steps forward solemnly.* ANNOUNCER *and* YOUNG WOMAN *leave the stage as he speaks*)

JUNIOR. (*Dramatic*) Gosh, what an honor. I don't know what to say. So many memories. (*Wipes away a tear*) Thanks, Mom. Thanks, Dad. Thanks, Grandpa, thanks, Grandma. (*He waves the doll to heaven*) I want to thank all the kids from Baboon High back in Upstate New York. They had faith in me when I was first starting out to be a winner. (*Waves*) Thanks, brother and sister baboons. (*Wipes away another tear*) What more can I say, except—I'm humble, humble . . . humble. (*He bows his head.* TREMENDOUS APPLAUSE, *etc. from the wings.* LIGHTS *return to normal.* CARMEL *has lived every minute of the vision*)

CARMEL. (*Clapping*) That's a wonderful dream. Fantasy-wise.

JUNIOR. Won't be a fantasy when it comes true.

CARMEL.. Didn't you forget something? Best screenplay.

JUNIOR. That's right. Best screenplay—*Disasterama* by Plato Voltaire.

CARMEL. Plato Voltaire!

JUNIOR. (*Makes a small gesture with his fingers to indicate size of tiny print*) Additional dialogue by Carmel McGregor.

CARMEL. Additional dialogue.

JUNIOR. Don't take it so hard, kid. They'll be other screenplays for you. (CARMEL *is close to the breaking point. She rages at* JUNIOR)

CARMEL. You monster! You conceited boor! You rat!

JUNIOR. What's the matter?

CARMEL. For months I've been locked in here typing script after script, living on junk food, hardly ever seeing another human being! And you tell me my reward is—*additional dialogue!*

JUNIOR. That's Hollywood, kid. The breaks. Think of it as mud-in-your-eye.

CARMEL. You think of this as pie-in-your face! (*She grabs a cream pie* from some container and pushes it into* JUNIOR'S *face*) I quit! (CARMEL *storms out,* LEFT. JUNIOR *is left standing with the meringue dripping down his chin. He tastes some*)

JUNIOR. Hmmmmm. Banana cream. My favorite.

---

*All that's necessary is a paper plate filled with shaving cream or whipped cream.

CURTAIN

END OF ACT TWO

ACT THREE

Scene 1

Before the lights come up on curtain, we hear the SHOUTS, YELLS, APPLAUSE *of movie fans.* ON LIGHTS UP *we see a group of fans and tourists grouped* EXTREME DOWN LEFT, *behind a rope or wooden barrier, waving autograph books and pencils, etc.*

SYLVIA METROLAND *stands* DOWN RIGHT, *a hand mike in her grip.* CAMERA OPERATOR *with a hand-held camera to her right,* DOWNSTAGE.

SYLVIA. Here we are, fans of movieland lore, way out in Pomona, California, in the lobby of Rabinowitz's Shanghai Palace, where the new film *Disasterama* is having its sneak preview. (*Fans cheer*) It's like an opening night, only no one knows about it. Secrecy is very important to a sneak. (*Loud cheer from fans as they look* RIGHT) Ah, here's the first of our bewitching stars, America's top funny lady—*Chuckles Lafoon.* (CHUCKLES ENTERS. *More cheers and applause.* NOTE: *Cheers, applause, etc. will be repeated wherever a star* ENTERS. *As each star leaves* SYLVIA *and* CROSSES LEFT *to enter the theatre, he or she will stop briefly to sign an autograph.* NOTE: CHUCKLES *has one arm in a sling. As other stars appear they, too, will show signs of some skirmish. One might be on a crutch, one might have an eye patch, another might be pushed on in a wheelchair, etc. See Suggestions*)
CHUCKLES. Ha, ha, ha.
SYLVIA. Chuckles, won't you say something to the mike?
CHUCKLES. Hi, Mike. Ha, ha, ha.
SYLVIA. I see your arm's in a sling. Is the rumor true?

CHUCKLES. Rumor?

SYLVIA. My spies tell me there was a near-riot at the cast party. Several stars of *Disasterama* were taken to emergency hospital.

CHUCKLES. We only went there to cheer up the patients.

SYLVIA. Hollywood has a big heart.

CHUCKLES. Tell you one thing. If Bronco Whinny throws another boot at me, I'm going to put axle grease on his saddle. Ha, ha, ha. The least he could have done is take off the spur. (*She moves* LEFT. THEO ENTERS)

SYLVIA. The star of all the great horror films—*Theo Bartok!* Theo, won't you say a few words to your devoted fans? (THEO *draws himself in great dignity, tosses the cape over one shoulder*)

THEO. No. (*He strides* LEFT. SYLVIA *is momentarily flustered, quickly recovers*)

SYLVIA. Look who's coming now! The glamorous Gee-Gee Fontaine and her leading man—Flint Wormwood. (*They* ENTER, *followed by* GEE-GEE's MAID, *who carries the chest of jewelry*) Gee-Gee, this is a fabulous night.

GEE-GEE. Real fab. (*Something she's taken a long time to memorize*) Unforgettable . . . unique . . . inspiring. *Disasterama* is the film of the rejuvenation.

SYLVIA. Rejuvenation? (GEE-GEE *looks perplexed, turns to* FLINT. *He whispers something in her ear*)

GEE-GEE. *Disasterama* is the film of the *generation*. (GEE-GEE *and* MAID *move* LEFT. *When* GEE-GEE *reaches fans, she distributes baubles, bangles and beads*)

SYLVIA. I understand this film is a bit of a departure for you, Flint. You actually get to kiss your leading lady.

FLINT. I don't want my fans to get the wrong idea. Flint Wormwood hasn't gone soft in the headplate. He's playing the field. Tough, rugged, macho, honcho.

SYLVIA. The qualities that have made Flint Wormwood a household word.

FLINT. If you're talking about "The Big House"— San Quentin. (*He moves* CENTER, *quickly whips out his police identification, draws his weapon*) "Freeze! You have the right to remain silent. If you give up the right to remain silent anything you say may and will be used against you in a court of law." (*Fans go wild. Shouts, yells, "Hey, Flint," "Go, Flint, go," "Nail 'em, Flint, baby."* BOB EVERLOVE ENTERS, *racquet in hand, escorting* BABY BERNICE. MRS. BUMBLE *behind them*)

SYLVIA. Look who's here. America's new child star— Baby Bernice Bumble. (*Makes a sour face*) Isn't she adorable? (BABY BERNICE *moves to microphone, curtsies, smiles*) Was working in this film difficult for you, Baby Bernice?

BABY BERNICE. Making this picture was no different than playing with my doll house. When I grow up I want to be a nurse.

SYLVIA. (*As fans applaud*) Isn't that commendable? America's sweetheart, I predict it. Who's your escort, as if I didn't know.

BABY BERNICE. (*Giggles childishly*) When I grow up I'm going to marry the boy next door.

MRS. BUMBLE. She's so wholesome.

BOB. (*All teeth*) When I heard Baby Bernice didn't have an escort for tonight's snake preview—

SYLVIA. —sneak, not snake—

BOB. —I said to myself, "Bob, you do something nice for someone else. You escort Baby Bernice and her mother, Mrs. Bumble of Bumble's Bank of Burbank, to the snake."

SYLVIA. Sneak. (*Trio moves* LEFT, *etc.*) There he goes, Bob Everlove, exhibiting all the charm that has won him a place in America's heart. (BRONCO *plods* IN)

BRONCO. I git the feelin' this hyar picture show is gonna be mah last roundup.

SYLVIA. Going to be a big box office hit, Bronco?

BRONCO. Yup.

SYLVIA. Bigger than your last film?

BRONCO. Yup.

SYLVIA. Going to make another film soon?

BRONCO. Nope.

SYLVIA. (*Surprised*) What are you going to do?

BRONCO. I'm going into politics.

SYLVIA. Politics?

BRONCO. I figured I've been so successful shootin' from

the hip, I might as well try shootin' from the lip. (*He Crosses Left*)

SYLVIA. Fabulous personality, fabulous. The one and only Bronco Ninny. (*Corrects herself*) Whinny. Ah, here's the director himself. Plato Voltaire.

VOLTAIRE. (ENTERS) I predict this film of *mine* will cause an international sensation. I have combined, in *my* film, all the techniques of the great cinema directors, of which I am number one. *Disasterama,* a film by Plato Voltaire, will stun the critics.

SYLVIA. Will you object to criticism?

VOLTAIRE. Plato Voltaire's too big to object. I will accept all criticism of *my* film, as long as it's out-and-out approval. (EXITS LEFT, *refusing autographs*)

SYLVIA. A fabulous director. That's it, Joe. Better wrap it up. (SYLVIA *and* CAMERA OPERATOR CROSS LEFT *to enter theatre. Fans also* EXIT)

FANS' AD LIBS.

I love disaster films!

I bet it's going to be great!

Flint Wormwood kisses?

Look what Gee-Gee Fontaine gave me.

How much is popcorn?

Does Rabinowitz validate?

Etc.

(*As the last of the mob trails into the theatre,* APASSIONATTA SWEEPS IN RIGHT)

APASSIONATTA. I'm ready for my interview, Miz Metroland. (*She stands, posing, wondering why nothing is happening, looks about, realizes no one is paying her any attention*) *You cretins! The best is always last! Everybody knows that!* (ETHEL ENTERS RIGHT, *worried*) I want a word with Junior. Where is he?

ETHEL. Everything's gone wrong.

APASSSIONATTA. I want Junior to reprimand Miz Metroland. Imagine, not interviewing the star.

ETHEL. No one was supposed to know about this sneak preview. Everyone's acting as if it's opening night.

APASSIONATTA. Wherever I am, it's opening night.

ETHEL. I don't know how Sylvia Metroland and the others found out.

APASSIONATTA. I do. I told them.

ETHEL. How did you know?

APASSIONATTA. Mister Rabinowitz is a long-time fan. Do you think he would allow Junior to have all the glory of this night? Impossible. When the film is over, my career takes off. Like a rocketship. (*She* EXITS LEFT)

ETHEL. (*Aside*) Pointed downward. (JUNIOR HURRIES IN, RIGHT)

JUNIOR. Find out anything? (ETHEL *points to the exiting* APASSIONATTA) You mean she knew about the sneak?

ETHEL. You got it on the first guess.

JUNIOR. Keep calm.

ETHEL. How can I keep calm when I'm terrified? You actually think they're going to thank you when they see what you've done?

JUNIOR. Yeah—when they see what a good picture we've got.

ETHEL. One of us is coo-coo and I'm beginning to think it's me. Let's go in and get it over with.

JUNIOR. I'll stay out here and pace.

ETHEL. (CROSSES LEFT) Wise decision. Why do I feel like I'm going to the guillotine? (*As* ETHEL EXITS LEFT *and* JUNIOR RIGHT, *the* LIGHTS *on the* FORESTAGE FADE To BLACK *and, then* SLOWLY DIM UP *somewhat and* FLICKER *to give the effect of a projector's glow. Slowly the* CURTAIN OPENS *only partway to reveal all the stars, plus* MRS. BUMBLE *and* VOLTAIRE *seated in two rows staring dumbly out into the audience. They are, supposedly, seated in the theatre watching the last of* Disasterama *which is represented by the flicker-light on the* FORESTAGE. *Needless to say, they are stunned, dazed, aghast.* GEE-GEE *has a giant box of popcorn. No one speaks for several seconds, then*)

BABY BERNICE. I'm not even in this picture!

GEE-GEE. Anyone would think I was a bit player!

VOLTAIRE. Who has ruined my masterpiece!

FLINT. What a piece of junk!

THEO. If this horror film is shown to the public, I'm ruined!

BRONCO. Could hurt my chances of being elected governor!

MRS. BUMBLE. I'll sue!

BOB. Who's responsible?

APASSIONATTA. Need you ask? That fiend in human form—*Junior Dover, Junior!*

FLINT. I'll knock his brains out!

CHUCKLES. You'll have to find them first!

BRONCO. What are we waitin' fer? Let's git the varmint!

BOB. Good idea!

THEO. He's probably slinking around in the lobby!

BABY BERNICE. I'll tell my daddy!

CHUCKLES. Get him with your spurs, Bronco! (*All get up, enraged, move* LEFT)

AD LIBS.

What a turkey of a movie!

My reputation! Ruined!

Call my lawyer!

Greta! Greta!

Where's Junior!

Let me have the first kick!

Don't let him get away!

Etc.

(*As they charge* OFF, CURTAINS CLOSE *and* LIGHTS UP FULL ON FORESTAGE. ETHEL *runs in from* LEFT)

ETHEL. Junior! Junior! (JUNIOR *runs* IN, RIGHT, *rubbing his hands in glee, convinced he's got a "hit"*)

JUNIOR. It's over?

ETHEL. You can say that again.

JUNIOR. How'd it go? Great, huh?

ETHEL. You'd better get out of here. Fast.

JUNIOR. Why?

ETHEL. Don't ask questions. Move! (ETHEL *turns, sees the others storming* IN *from* LEFT) Too late.

AD LIBS.

There he is!

Let me at him!

Monster!

I'll strangle you!

You creep!

Etc.

JUNIOR. (*Innocently*) Didn't you like the movie? (*Howl of outrage*)

BRONCO. (*Rolling up his sleeves*) Pardner, I'm tearing you limb from limb.

FLINT. When I'm done with you they'll have to sop you up with a sponge.

CHUCKLES. You're something from the jungle, kid. I bet you're the first member of your family who was raised in captivity.

GEE-GEE. Give me back the cufflinks.

AD LIBS.

How could you!

You liar!

I'll see you in court!

Etc.

JUNIOR. If you'll only let me explain. (GRETA ENTERS LEFT, *pushes her way through the mob*)

GRETA. Let me in there, let me through.

JUNIOR. Glad you could make it, Greta.

GRETA. Don't you "glad-you-could-make-it-Greta" me. Do you realize you had two of the top grossers in the country in your picture, and you have them on film for about five minutes each!

JUNIOR. Nothing to get excited about.

GRETA. Nothing to get excited about! There I was in the balcony waiting for Bob Everlove and Flint Wormwood to do their stuff and before I could sneeze they were gone.

JUNIOR. I can explain everything.

THEO. You can't explain what we saw in that theatre. Trash. It was crude and vulgar. I wouldn't work for you again for a million dollars.

ETHEL. No, you'd do it for a lot less.

THEO. I'm going to see you in a pin-stripe suit. Prison stripe.

MRS. BUMBLE. You have much to answer for, young man. I wouldn't like to be in your shoes.

JUNIOR. They probably wouldn't fit. Look, everyone, it was a sneak preview. There are a few things that need to be changed here and there, I admit—

MRS. BUMBLE. Baby Bernice wasn't in a single frame. You'll hear from my solicitor in the morning.

JUNIOR. Trust me. Everything's going to be fine.

APASSIONATTA. Don't believe a word of it. I'll tell you what he's been up to. (ETHEL *moves, nervously, to* JUNIOR) He's given each of you a different script, one in which you would star. What he wanted to do was to get as many stars in his picture as possible. He never had any intention of making any kind of film except that mish-mash we saw on the screen.

GRETA. (*Growls*) Is that true?

JUNIOR. Well, uh, not exactly.

APASSIONATTA. Liar. (*The mob advances on* JUNIOR)

ETHEL. Junior will fix everything.

FLINT. I wish I had real bullets in my magnum.

ETHEL. (*As they advance*) What are we going to do?

JUNIOR. (*Shaking*) I don't know what you're going to do, but I know what I'm going to do.

ETHEL. What?

JUNIOR. *Run!!!* (*He turns, flees* RIGHT. ETHEL *follows. Others charge in pursuit*)

AD LIBS.
    Come back!
    Don't let him get away!
    Get him!
    Follow him!
    Tackle him!
    Get the police!
    Etc.

(*In one angry wave, they sweep after* JUNIOR *bent on vegeance.* LIGHTS FADE FAST TO BLACKOUT. *A few seconds pass.* SPOTLIGHT HITS DOWN LEFT. WINIFRED LUNG *and* SCRIPT PERSON ENTER. SCRIPT PERSON *has a newspaper.* WINIFRED *dabs away a tear with a hanky*)

WINIFRED. What else does it say?

SCRIPT PERSON. Not much.

WINIFRED. The first paragraph again.

SCRIPT PERSON. "All filmland is wondering what has become of Junior Dover, Junior. Not seen since the screening of his film, *Disasterama*, several weeks ago, in Pomona. Authorities are beginning to fear the worst."

WINIFRED. (*Sighs*) Alas, poor Junior. All those lawsuits against him. I suppose it was too great a burden. If only I had been kinder to him.

SCRIPT PERSON. "Police are dragging Movieland Lake where Mister Dover, Junior, was last observed, patting a stray puppy."

WINIFRED. How like Junior. His last moments a dog. Let us observe a moment of silence. In his memory. (WINIFRED *and* SCRIPT PERSON *bow heads reverently.* WINIFRED *immediately lifts her head*) That's enough. I wonder if you could give me a lift to the social security office? (*They* EXIT, SPOTLIGHT OUT)

CURTAIN

ACT THREE

SCENE 2

The sound stage, DIMLY LIGHTED. CURTAIN SLOWLY OPENS. *A moment passes and* GINGER ENTERS, *surreptitiously,* DOWN RIGHT. *She carries a box of food.*

GINGER. Pssssst. Miz Kent. (*No reply. She steps* CENTER) Miz Kent. It's me. Ginger. (ETHEL ENTERS UP LEFT)

ETHEL. Anyone see you come in?

GINGER. No, not a soul. I came in through the small gate at the back of the lot. The one you gave me the key to. There's a security man in front. (ETHEL *takes box*) How long do you think Mister Dover, Junior, will have to hide out?

ETHEL. Anybody's guess.

GINGER. The papers say he has a ten-million-dollar lawsuit against him.

ETHEL. For starters.

GINGER. Let me know if there's anything else I can do to help. I liked working for him. It's interesting working for a kook. You don't get bored.

ETHEL. I know what you mean.

GINGER. Give me a call if you need anything else.

ETHEL. Thanks, Ginger.

GINGER. (EXITS RIGHT) Any time. (ETHEL *puts box on table*)

ETHEL. Dinner time. (*Cautiously,* JUNIOR *appears from* UP LEFT *wearing a ridiculous false beard*)

JUNIOR. What am I having?

ETHEL. Same as yesterday. Take-out chicken.

JUNIOR. (*Sits at table*) I've eaten so much take-out chicken, I'm beginning to cluck.

ETHEL. That phony chin spinach won't fool anyone.

JUNIOR. You think I'd be recognized?

ETHEL. I don't think it. I know it. Eat. (*She sits beside him.* JUNIOR *digs into the box, comes up with a chicken leg*)

JUNIOR. Ethel, I was thinking—

ETHEL. —optimist—

JUNIOR. —I'm being serious. I could be a pretty good salesman. There's a lot of money to be made in used cars. Rugs, too. People everywhere are crying out for rugs.

ETHEL. I don't see you as a used car salesman. Or a rug merchant.

JUNIOR. I'll have to do something.

ETHEL. You're a movieman. It's in your blood, like a crazy germ. If you'd only trust your talent instead of thinking up crazy schemes.

JUNIOR. I believed in *Disasterama*. (*Shakes his head*) It would take a miracle to salvage it.

ETHEL. Anything can happen.

JUNIOR. Yeah. I could end up behind bars. Probably will.

ETHEL. There's something I think I ought to tell you. Maybe you'll be pleased, maybe you won't.

JUNIOR. What's the mystery. (VOICES *of* PAULINE *and* SALLY *from* DOWN LEFT)

PAULINE. (OFFSTAGE) Miz Kent!

SALLY. (OFFSTAGE) Miz Kent!

JUNIOR. (*Startled*) Who's that!

ETHEL. It's all right. Pauline and Sally. They know we're here.

JUNIOR. Who?

ETHEL. You remember. They worked with Baby Bernice.

JUNIOR. Don't say that name. I'm eating. I'd better duck out of sight. (*He starts to* EXIT UP RIGHT. *Darts back for rest of his dinner,* EXITS. SALLY *and* PAULINE, *excited,* ENTER DOWN LEFT. SALLY *carries a stack of newspapers*)

SALLY. It worked!

PAULINE. Better than we hoped! You were right, Miz Kent.

ETHEL. (*Points to papers*) Reviews?

SALLY. The first of them. Read the top one. Second page. (ETHEL *stands, takes the paper, opens it, reads*)

ETHEL. "Yesterday's official opening of the latest Junior Dover, Junior film *The Great All-American Musical Disaster* will take its place in the annuals of film-making as one of the most original and amusing epics ever made." (*Joyous*) Whoopee! I can't believe it!

PAULINE. The others are even better. (JUNIOR *rushes back in*)

JUNIOR. Let me see that! (*He grabs the paper from* ETHEL, *reads*) "A masterwork of cinema art." (*He grabs another paper, finds another review*) "*Great All-American Disaster* Wins Applause." (*Another paper, opens*) "Baby Bernice Bumble Greatest Find Since Uranium." I'd better sit down before I fall down. (*He sits*) I don't get it.

ETHEL. The picture was there all the time. You didn't know where to look for it.

SALLY. Miz Kent said it couldn't do any harm to do what we did.

PAULINE. So we thought we'd do it.

JUNIOR. *Do what!*

SALLY. She suggested we take all those bits of film we made with Baby Bernice singing and dancing, and insert them in the footage you worked on.

JUNIOR. Wait a minute. (*Reads further in review*) "The idea of uniting the disaster theme with the musical inanities of a child prodigy not only works marvelously well, but makes this film one of the funniest of the year.

Everyone in the cast is a fine comic talent." I made a serious film.

ETHEL. You only thought you did. This lets you off the hook.

JUNIOR. They still want my chicken neck.

SALLY. I don't think so, Mister Dover, Junior. Apassionatta Abalone was on the television this morning being interviewed. She said it was a great honor to be in the film.

JUNIOR. I don't believe it.

ETHEL. They hated you when the picture was a bomb. They love you now that it's a hit.

PAULINE. I hope we did right.

JUNIOR. You did. You saved the picture. You saved the studio. You saved me.

SALLY. No, about telling them you were here.

JUNIOR. Who? (HUBBUB *of* NOISE *from* OFF-LEFT *and* OFF-RIGHT. *Junior stands*)
AD LIBS.

> Someone turn up the lights!
> Where is that dear boy!
> I always said Junior was a crafty fellow!
> A genius!
> Junior, where are you?
> Bravo!

(*At this point all the* STARS, *plus* MRS. BUMBLE, VOLTAIRE *are in, grouped for the best stage picture. As they enter,* LIGHTS UP FULL)

VOLTAIRE. That beard. Wonderful. I see you as the Count of Monte Cristo.

MRS. BUMBLE. You were right, Junior. We should have trusted you. The film is brilliant. The audience loves it. The critics love it. My husband says it will make a fortune.

GRETA. (OFF STAGE) Let me through there, let me in. (*She* ENTERS DOWN RIGHT, *pushes her way to* JUNIOR) Have I got a script for you. If you make it half as good as *The Great All-American Musical Disaster*, we're set for life. (CARMEL, *looking confident and self-assured,* ENTERS DOWN RIGHT)

JUNIOR. I have a script writer. (*Nods*) Carmel McGregor.

ETHEL. I think you ought to know. We gave Carmel the screen credit.   ˋ

VOLTAIRE. I got "additional dialogue." Who cares? Every studio in town is asking for my services.

CHUCKLES. Television's loss is the movies' loss. Ha, ha, ha.

GEE-GEE. You can keep the cufflinks, Junior.

JUNIOR. Gee, Gee-Gee, thanks.

GEE-GEE. The *Los Angeles Times* says I was never better than in your film. They didn't realize I was such a comedienne.

SALLY. We didn't dub her voice.

BRONCO. I can pick up a heap of votes with this hyar picture. My name is gonna be up there on all the marquees. Voter identification. Can't buy publicity like that. Nope.

THEO. Critics are referring to me as "The Laughing Vampire." This film will open up a whole new area for me.

FLINT. Have to admit I looked pretty good up there. Never realized I was a comedian, either.

CHUCKLES. That makes two of us. Ha, ha, ha.

APASSIONATTA. (*Steps to* JUNIOR) Silence! I only want to say that I, Apassionatta Abalone, had faith in this film from the beginning. It was I who recognized its potential and offered to accept any role, no matter how small, just to share modestly in its success. (SYLVIA METROLAND ENTERS DOWN LEFT, *pencil ready*)

SYLVIA. Junior, you've done it! It's Academy Awards all the way. I knew you could pull it off.

JUNIOR. I guess I don't go to jail.

MRS. BUMBLE. Certainly not. The world of film needs you.

BOB. What do you say, neighbor? Forgive and forget? (*Long pause, then:*)

JUNIOR. Why not? (*Mighty* CHEER *goes up, applause, etc.* BOB *and* JUNIOR *shake hands*)

GRETA. Let's get down to business. Another Baby Bumble film should start filming as soon as possible. We don't want to lose momentum. Let me tell you about the script.

JUNIOR. I told you, Carmel's my writer.

GRETA. She was. Not only has she joined the Writers Guild, she's my client. And she doesn't work cheap.

CARMEL. It's a good script. Junior. Winner-wise.

GRETA. Can we work out a deal?

JUNIOR. Why not? After all, THIS IS HOLLYWOOD!

ALL. Anything can happen! (*Taking this as her cue,* BABY BERNICE *bounces* CENTER, *curtsies, sings, dances.* REST OF CAST ENTERS, LEFT *and* RIGHT. ALL *join in the singing*)

ENTIRE CAST. (*Lively*)

ANYTHING CAN HAPPEN, TRULY
ANYTHING AT ALL
IF YOU ONLY KEEP ON SMILING
SUMMER, SPRING AND FALL.

IF YOU'LL ONLY STAY WITH LAUGHTER
ETC.

CURTAIN

END OF PLAY

PRODUCTION NOTES

PROPERTIES, ACT ONE: Long table with scripts, chair; desk with chair, telephone, dressing screen with movie posters, sofa.

Scene 1, BROUGHT ON: Wristwatch (ETHEL), messages (GINGER), scripts (CARMEL), pad and pencil (SYLVIA), long cigarette holder, script (CHUCKLES), guitar and script (BRONCO), paper (APASSIONATTA), Teddy Bear (BABY BERNICE).

Scene 2, BROUGHT ON: Papers, bell (SYLVIA), costume sketches (GINGER), script, riding crop (VOLTAIRE), small chest with jewelry (GEE-GEE's MAID), long contract "roll" or window shade, pen (GRETA), tennis racquet (BOB).

ACT TWO: Scene 1, Sound Stage: Tables (3) with chairs, high bushy plants, dressing table with chair, makeup table with bench or chair, director's chair, standing camera. BROUGHT ON: Maps, sandwich board reading: MAPS TO THE STARS' HOMES (MAP SELLER), cameras (TOURISTS), clapboard and chalk (ASSISTANT DIRECTOR), apple (APASSIONATTA), holster, gun (FLINT), whistle (VOLTAIRE), script (SCRIPT PERSON), powder puff with heavy dusting of powder (MAKEUP ARTIST)—or puff can be placed on makeup table prior to curtain, sea captain's hat (THEO).

Scene 2, Table or desk, high stool, typewriter, scripts, overflowing wastebaskets, food containers, one with "stage pie." BROUGHT ON: Bell (SYLVIA, ANNOUNCER), tray with small dolls, envelopes.

69

ACT THREE: Rope oɪ wooden barrier, benches for theatre seats.

Scene 1: BROUGHT ON: Autograph books, pencils, hand camera, hand mike, assorted "injury props" (optional)—crutch, wheelchair, eye patch, etc., tennis racquet (BOB), police badge, pistol and holster (FLINT), jewelry box with jewelry (MAID), box of popcorn (GEE-GEE).

Scene 2, Sound Stage setting. BROUGHT ON: Hanky (WINIFRED), box with chicken leg (GINGER), newspapers (SALLY), pad and pencil (SYLVIA).

SOUND EFFECTS

Telephone, wind and rain: storm effects, BOOM of meteorite, applause, musical fanfare or drum roll. The wind and rain effects (Sound record No. 1026) and the drum roll (Sound record No. 1024) available from Baker's Plays.

LIGHTING EFFECTS

Area lighting as indicated in script. Use as best fits the individual stage. Flickering effect to suggest a movie picture being projected, meteorite flash.

COSTUMES

Described in script, as characters make initial entrance. However, imagination will play a big part here. The costumes should be bright and colorful giving an "almost circus" aura. If desired, characters can have different costumes for different scenes. For example, at the "Sneak Preview" the women might be in evening gowns or the latest "fad" style. The costuming is completely flexible. Can be as fanciful as director wishes or as minimal.

ON CASTING: Any number of roles can be played by either actor or actress (TV ANNOUNCER, MAP SELLER, TOURIST GUIDE, ASSISTANT DIRECTOR, SCRIPT PERSON, MAKEUP ARTIST, MUSICIAN, etc.) The smaller roles can also double as TOURISTS, FANS, etc.

Special attention should be given to casting the role of ETHEL KENT. She is the one "sane" note in with the madness, the "voice of reason" that much of the nonsense will play against.

OTHER TITLES AVAILABLE FROM SAMUEL FRENCH

TAKE HER, SHE'S MINE

Phoebe and Henry Ephron

Comedy / 11m, 6f / Various Sets

Art Carney and Phyllis Thaxter played the Broadway roles of parents of two typical American girls enroute to college. The story is based on the wild and wooly experiences the authors had with their daughters, Nora Ephron and Delia Ephron, themselves now well known writers. The phases of a girl's life are cause for enjoyment except to fearful fathers. Through the first two years, the authors tell us, college girls are frightfully sophisticated about all departments of human life. Then they pass into the "liberal" period of causes and humanitarianism, and some into the intellectual lethargy of beatniksville. Finally, they start to think seriously of their lives as grown ups. It's an experience in growing up, as much for the parents as for the girls.

"A warming comedy. A delightful play about parents vs kids. It's loaded with laughs. It's going to be a smash hit."
– *New York Mirror*

OTHER TITLES AVAILABLE FROM SAMUEL FRENCH

MURDER AMONG FRIENDS
Bob Barry

Comedy Thriller / 4m, 2f / Interior

Take an aging, exceedingly vain actor; his very rich wife; a double dealing, double loving agent, plunk them down in an elegant New York duplex and add dialogue crackling with wit and laughs, and you have the basic elements for an evening of pure, sophisticated entertainment. Angela, the wife and Ted, the agent, are lovers and plan to murder Palmer, the actor, during a contrived robbery on New Year's Eve. But actor and agent are also lovers and have an identical plan to do in the wife. A murder occurs, but not one of the planned ones.

"Clever, amusing, and very surprising."
– *New York Times*

"A slick, sophisticated show that is modern and very funny."
– WABC TV

OTHER TITLES AVAILABLE FROM SAMUEL FRENCH

THE RIVERS AND RAVINES
Heather McDonald

Drama / 9m, 5f / Unit Set
Originally produced to acclaim by Washington D.C.'s famed
Arena Stage. This is an engrossing political drama about the
contemporary farm crisis in America and its effect on rural
communities.

"A haunting and emotionally draining play. A community of
farmers and ranchers in a small Colorado town disintegrates
under the weight of failure and thwarted ambitions. Most of
the farmers, their spouses, children, clergyman, banker and
greasy spoon proprietress survive, but it is survival without
triumph. This is an *Our Town* for the 80's."
– *The Washington Post*

www.ingramcontent.com/pod-product-compliance
Lightning Source LLC
Chambersburg PA
CBHW070357120726
47909CB00008B/2885